Step into the world of NYC Angels

Looking out over Central Park, the Angel Mendez Children's Hospital, affectionately known as Angel's, is famed throughout America for being at the forefront of pediatric medicine, with talented staff who always go that extra mile for their little patients. Their lives are full of highs, lows, drama and emotion.

In the city that never sleeps, the lifesaving docs at Angel's Hospital work hard, play hard and love even harder. There's *always* time for some sizzling after-hours romance….

And striding the halls of the hospital, leaving a sea of fluttering hearts behind him, is the dangerously charismatic new head of neurosurgery, Alejandro Rodriguez. But there's one woman, pediatrician Layla Woods, who's left an indelible mark on his no-go-area heart.
Expect their reunion to be explosive!

NYC Angels

Children's doctors who work hard and love even harder…in the city that never sleeps!

Dear Reader,

I need one of those T-shirts that say I love New York! Visiting the Big Apple is fun as there are so many things to do and to see. I especially like seeing Broadway plays, the Statue of Liberty and jogging in Central Park (just to name a few).

So I was thrilled and honored when I was asked to participate in the NYC Angels series by writing the third book.

Dan Morris is a top-notch pediatric cardiothoracic surgeon who meets his match in physical therapist Molly Shriver. Molly makes it clear she is the one running the show when it comes to helping Dan's son, Josh, to walk again.

Both Dan and Molly have been burned by relationships in the past, but as they work together for Josh's sake, is it possible they'll get a second chance at love and family?

I hope you enjoy Dan and Molly's story as much as I enjoyed writing it. Don't hesitate to visit my website or find me on Facebook—I love to hear from my readers.

Sincerely

Laura Iding

www.LauraIding.com

NYC ANGELS: UNMASKING DR. SERIOUS

Laura Iding

HARLEQUIN® MEDICAL ROMANCE™

To the Thursday Morning Breakfast Club. I value your support more than I can ever say.

ISBN-13: 978-0-373-06883-8

NYC ANGELS: UNMASKING DR. SERIOUS

First North American Publication 2013

Recycling programs for this product may not exist in your area.

Printed in U.S.A.

www.Harlequin.com

NYC Angels

*Children's doctors who work hard and love even harder...
in the city that never sleeps!*

**Step into the world of NYC Angels and enjoy
two new stories a month**

Last month, New York's most notoriously sinful bachelor, Jack Carter,
found a woman he wanted to spend more than just one night with in

NYC ANGELS: REDEEMING THE PLAYBOY by Carol Marinelli

And reluctant socialite Eleanor Aston made the gossip headlines
when the paparazzi discovered her baby bombshell in

NYC ANGELS: HEIRESS'S BABY SCANDAL by Janice Lynn

This month, cheery physiotherapist Molly Shriver melts the icy
barricades around hotshot surgeon Dan Morris's damaged heart in

NYC ANGELS: UNMASKING DR. SERIOUS by Laura Iding

And Lucy Edwards is finally tempted to let neurosurgeon
Ryan O'Doherty in. But their fragile relationship will need to survive
her most difficult revelation yet....

NYC ANGELS: THE WALLFLOWER'S SECRET by Susan Carlisle

Then, in May, newly single (and strictly off-limits!) Chloe Jenkins
makes it very difficult for drop-dead-gorgeous Brad Davis
to resist temptation!

NYC ANGELS: FLIRTING WITH DANGER by Tina Beckett

And after meeting single dad Lewis Jackson, tough-cookie head
nurse Scarlet Miller wonders if she's finally met her match....

NYC ANGELS: TEMPTING NURSE SCARLET by Wendy S. Marcus

Finally join us in June, when bubbly new nurse Polly Seymour is the
ray of sunshine that brooding doc Johnny Griffin needs in

NYC ANGELS: MAKING THE SURGEON SMILE by Lynne Marshall

And Alex Rodriguez and Layla Woods come back into each other's
orbit, trying to fool the buzzing hospital grapevine that the spark
between them has died. But can they convince each other?

NYC ANGELS: AN EXPLOSIVE REUNION by Alison Roberts

**Be captivated by NYC Angels in this new eight-book continuity
from Harlequin® Medical™ Romance.**

**These books are also available in ebook format from
www.Harlequin.com.**

CHAPTER ONE

"No-o-o-o!" Josh wailed, throwing his arms around the nanny's neck when Dan tried to lift the boy off the sofa. "I want Gemma to take me!"

Dan Morris gnashed his teeth, his gut burning with guilt as Josh showed him once again how much he preferred the company of Gemma, the middle-aged woman who'd been caring for him the past six months, over that of his father. But with the ease of long practice he buried his true feelings and kept his tone soft as he gently prised Josh away from Gemma, lifting his small frame into his arms.

"It's okay, Josh. Remember how I told you I'm going to be home with you for the next few weeks? We're going to attend physical therapy together. There's nothing to be afraid of. I'm going to be with you the whole time."

Josh didn't look too impressed with his

vow but thankfully stopped struggling, leaning against his father's chest as if willing to accept his fate. He'd stopped crying too, but the occasional loud sniffle was just as difficult to bear.

Dan tucked Josh into his booster seat in the backseat of the black BMW, buckling him securely into the harness before he himself slid into the driver's seat, trying to think of a way to breach the chasm between them. He wanted Josh to know he was loved. Cherished. But how? Words alone hadn't worked so far.

"Daddy, is therapy going to hurt?"

Helpless fury and guilt nearly choked him at his son's innocent question. How many times had Josh asked him that same thing in the hospital? How many times had he been forced to answer yes? He cleared his throat and smiled at Josh, using the rearview mirror. "No, Josh, therapy isn't going to hurt. The therapist will exercise your legs. There won't be any needles, I promise."

Josh settled back, seemingly reassured. Dan drove carefully through the busy Manhattan streets to the physiotherapy clinic located within the brick walls of Manhattan's Angel Mendez Children's Hospital, affectionately known as Angel's, where his pediatric cardiothoracic surgery practice was located. He hoped physical therapist Molly Shriver was everything she'd been reported to be.

He'd wanted the best, *demanded* the best for his son. He couldn't bear to think about the grim possibility that Josh might never walk again. If this Molly Shriver was half as good as her reputation heralded her to be, he was convinced she was the one who could make that happen.

He and Josh arrived ten minutes early because he despised being late. They'd barely settled into their seats in the waiting room when a young woman with bright green eyes and reddish-gold hair pulled back in a perky ponytail came out to greet them.

"Good morning," she said, smiling brightly, her attention focused, rightly so, on Josh. Dan had stood when she'd entered the room, but Josh was obviously still seated in the waiting-room chair, wearing shorts and a T-shirt as requested. She knelt beside Josh so that her eyes were level with his. "You must be Josh Morris, although you look much older than seven. Are you sure you're not eight or nine?" she asked, her voice full of doubt.

Josh giggled, and shook his head. "Nope. I'm seven but my birthday is in three weeks."

"Oh, goody! I love birthdays! We'll have a party to celebrate!" she exclaimed, making Josh giggle again. "And that must be why you look so much older. My name is Molly and I'm so happy you came in to see me today."

Dan tucked his hands into the back pockets of his jeans and watched, reluctantly impressed with how she'd immediately established a connection with his son. She seemed to know a lot about kids.

No doubt, far more than he did.

"We're going to have lots of fun today, Josh," Molly confided. She held out her hand to his son. "Are you ready to play some games with me?"

All evidence of his former tears gone, Josh nodded eagerly as he reached for her hand. Fearing that she didn't realize his son couldn't walk, Dan quickly swooped down to swing Josh into his arms. "We're ready," he said gruffly, sending her a dark look.

For a moment her gaze narrowed and her smile dimmed. "Did you leave Josh's wheelchair out in the car?" she asked with feigned sweetness.

Just the thought of seeing his son confined

to a wheelchair made him break out in a cold sweat. He could spend twelve hours in surgery, meticulously reconnecting coronary arteries and veins to repair tiny damaged hearts, but those hours he'd sat at his son's hospital bedside after the car crash had been the longest, darkest hours of his life. "No," he said bluntly. "Josh won't need a wheelchair. He has me. And now he has you, to help him learn how to walk again."

Her lips thinned and her smile faded even more. He thought she was going to pursue the issue, but instead she led the way through the doorway into another, much larger room. There were all kinds of exercise equipment scattered about, along with what appeared to be toys. Lots of toys, like brightly colored balls of every shape and size, jump ropes, bean bags and hula hoops. She gestured toward a padded table located on the right-hand side of the room. "Josh needs to sit right here. And why don't you take a seat here, on his left?"

He gently set Josh on the padded table, taken aback by how she wanted him right next to Josh, since he'd planned to just sit back and watch. "I can sit over there," he said, indicating a hard plastic chair tucked in the corner of the room.

"I'm afraid that won't work," Molly said cheerfully. "We'll need you close by in order to help. Right, Josh?"

"Right," Josh agreed enthusiastically, although Dan was sure the boy had no idea what he was agreeing to.

While it grated against his nerves to take orders from this petite woman, whose head barely reached the level of his chin, he'd vowed to do whatever was necessary for his son. And belatedly he realized she probably wanted to teach him the same exercises that she'd be doing with Josh, so he could reinforce them at home. "All right, then." He pulled up a rolling stool to sit close to his son's left side.

"Excellent." Molly grabbed a red plastic ball that was slightly smaller in circumference than a basketball, and took a seat on another rolling stool, positioning herself off to Josh's right side. "We're going to play catch, okay, Josh?"

He nodded enthusiastically.

"Watch carefully. I need you to toss the ball high in the air, like this…" She demonstrated what she meant, throwing her arms in the air and then keeping them over her head to catch the ball again. "And then catch it again like this. Are you ready?" she asked.

When Josh nodded, she tossed the ball in a high arch, so that Josh had to lift up his arms to catch it. "Great!" she called with enthusiasm. "Now toss it back up in the air toward your dad."

Before Dan realized what was happening, Josh did as she requested, the ball going high in the air and crookedly off to one side, so that Dan had to react quickly in order to catch it. He wanted to scowl at the obvious amusement in Molly's gaze, but as usual kept his feelings to himself. Besides, he found her enthusiasm and laughter oddly relaxing.

"Good job, Josh. Now, Mr. Morris, toss the ball back to your son."

It was on the tip of his tongue to correct her, *Dr. Morris, pediatric cardiothoracic surgeon,* but right now the focus needed to be on his son. He didn't mind taking the role of a concerned father. After all, he was currently on leave of absence from the hospital, with one of his partners covering his patients. "Dan," he said shortly, as he did as she requested, tossing the ball up in the air so his son could reach out for it. "Call me Dan."

She didn't answer, as if she couldn't have cared less what his name was, and her gaze remained trained on his son. He tried to squelch a flash of annoyance. "Now, throw the ball back up in the air, toward me, Josh," Molly said. "Up as high as you can."

This time Josh's aim was a little better, although the ball still veered off to the side. They repeated this game several times, and Dan couldn't help glancing at the clock with growing annoyance. Okay, maybe he could understand her need to establish a bond with his son, but was this really what their medical insurance was paying for? What good would tossing the ball in the air do for Josh's legs? When was she going to start with his muscle-strengthening exercises?

"Great job, Josh," Molly said with another broad, cheerful smile. She looked and acted as if she absolutely loved her job. "Okay, now we're going to work with a hacky sack." She put the red ball back on the shelf and brought over a small round beanbag. "Have you ever played with a hacky sack, Josh?"

"No," he said, a tiny frown furrowing his brow as he watched Molly. She tossed the hacky sack into the air and bounced it off her elbow, aiming up so that she could catch it again. Then she repeated the motion with the other elbow, and then with her knee.

It was on the tip of Dan's tongue to remind her, again, that his son couldn't walk or stand for any length of time to play the goofy game of hacky sack, but then she sat down on the rolling stool, still holding the small beanbag.

"This isn't an easy game, so you have to concentrate very hard," she warned. "Do you think you can do that for me?"

Josh's big brown eyes were wide as he nodded.

"Maybe we should get your dad to play, too," Molly said, with a mischievous glint in her eye. Without warning she tossed the hacky sack into the air and then bounced it off her elbow and then her knee, aiming toward him. She hit it hard enough to make him scramble to reach up and grab it before the beanbag could smack him in the center of his forehead.

His temper snapped as he tossed the hacky sack back in her lap. "Maybe you should quit playing games and get to work." The moment the sharp words left his mouth he wanted to call them back, especially when Josh's brown eyes darkened with wounded sorrow.

Slicing his heart like the sharp blade of a scalpel.

* * *

It took everything Molly had to keep her relaxed smile on her face, when in reality she wanted to sweep Josh into her arms and take him far away from his ogre of a father.

"Hmm, I think your dad got up on the wrong side of the bed this morning, Josh," she murmured, picking up the hacky sack and turning in her seat so that she faced Josh. She lowered her voice and leaned forward as if he was her coconspirator. "Or maybe it's just that he doesn't know how to play games," she said as if they were sharing a big secret. "You and I are going to have to help teach him, okay?"

Josh bit his lip and ducked his head, sending a worried glance at his father. "Okay," he said in a very small voice, as if torn between siding with her and trying to protect his father.

She did her best to ignore Dr. Morris's piercing gaze. She knew very well who he was, of course. After all, she'd seen him at the ribbon-cutting ceremony when Angel's had opened the new neonatal wing, although he hadn't noticed her. Plus, she'd cared for many patients who'd had surgery performed by him. Parents raved about what a great surgeon he was.

Dr. Morris had an amazing reputation within the hospital, but she couldn't say she was nearly as impressed with the guy in person. Granted, he was devastatingly attractive—tall and broad-shouldered, with mink-colored close-cropped hair and big, melting chocolate-brown eyes. But she wasn't easily swayed these days by a good-looking guy. Especially one who rarely, if ever, smiled.

In fact, they'd be far better off if he'd put his frowning energy into his son's therapy instead. She was still seething with the fact that he'd denied his son the freedom of a wheelchair.

But there would be time to talk to Dr. Morris about that later. Right now she needed to concentrate on poor Josh, who deserved every bit of her attention. "Okay, here's what I need you to do for me," she said with a smile and a secret wink. Josh rewarded her with a tremulous smile, so heartbreakingly sweet she had to crush the urge to sweep him into her arms and promise him that she'd never let anything bad happen to him.

Ridiculous, as Josh was her patient, not

part of her family. He belonged to the stern-faced surgeon sitting next to him. And she'd do well to remember that.

Don't get emotionally involved. You'll only lose another piece of your heart once this adorable little boy doesn't need you anymore.

She made a career out of helping her small patients not need her anymore. So, of course, she needed to keep a safe emotional distance from them. However, telling herself not to get emotionally involved was easier than actually doing it. Still, she gave it her best shot. "I want you to bounce the hacky sack in the air with your elbows and your knees." She demonstrated what she wanted him to do. "Now, you try it."

Josh did his best, which was more than she could say about his father, who watched him like a hawk. More than once he almost came out of his chair to help his son, even though she sent him a glance that clearly told him to back off.

Josh's ability was hampered a bit by the fact that he sat on the exam table, he would have done better in a wheelchair, but soon he managed to get a decent rhythm going. She was glad that he had the ability to move his knees because that meant his hips were in good shape.

"Excellent job," she lavishly praised him. "Now, let's try something else. Try to kick my hands with your toes. Kick me as hard as you can."

Josh tried to lift up his legs so that he could kick her hands, but his leg muscles were too weak. The bright angry red scars that marred his youthful skin weren't easy to ignore. But the weakness in his legs was even worse. She hid her dismay at how little he could raise them upward. He would need a lot of work to get his strength back.

Good thing she had plenty of patience. Unlike his father.

"Let's try something else," she quickly improvised, since he couldn't kick the palms of her hands. She reached over to lift him up and quickly set him down on the floor before Dr. Morris could jump up to take over. She grabbed the red plastic ball again and placed it between Josh's feet. "Try and kick the ball sideways toward your other foot, but keep your leg straight like this." She gently moved his right leg, showing him what she wanted him to do.

Josh did as she asked, shifting his right

leg enough to move the ball, although it went barely a few inches before rolling to a stop far away from his left foot.

"Great, that's wonderful, Josh." She quickly moved the ball so that it was located near his left foot. "Now, kick it back again."

He scrunched up his face with the effort to concentrate on doing what she'd asked. He tried a couple more times but only moved the ball scant inches. And suddenly he crumpled into tears. "I can't," he wailed. "I can't kick the b-ball!"

This time she did wrap her arms around him in comfort. How could she not? "Don't cry, please don't cry," she crooned softly. "You're doing very well, Josh. Remember how I said some of the games were hard? Believe me, very soon you'll be kicking that ball between your feet just fine. Just don't give up on me, okay? I promise we'll keep working on these games together. But I need you to do your part."

He quieted against her, and eventually nodded his head against her breast. She was relieved that Josh had got over his breakdown quickly—some patients took much longer, even her teenage patients. This type of frustration wasn't new to her by any means.

When she glanced up at Dr. Morris to reassure him that Josh's reaction was completely normal, she caught her breath at the starkness of his gaze as he stared at his son. Pain shadowed the brown depths, mixed with what appeared to be guilt and a hint of longing.

She took a deep breath and let it out slowly. Apparently Josh wasn't the only one who needed help. And no matter how much she wanted to, she couldn't turn her back on his father.

She could only hope and pray that she could get through this new challenge without too many emotional scars.

If it wasn't too late already.

CHAPTER TWO

BATTLING A WAVE of helplessness, Dan clenched his hands into tight fists, wishing he could be the one to comfort his son. But Josh didn't often turn to his father for comfort.

Because he hadn't been there enough for him. Not because he didn't want to be but because his career was demanding. His young patients didn't just need open heart surgery during the day. He was on call every third evening and every third weekend. And that meant he'd often been forced to leave Josh in the care of his nanny.

At least the nannies were better to Josh than his mother had been. Although that didn't stop Josh from asking for her, especially when he was stressed. Dan rubbed the ache at his temples. He hated knowing that his son was still suffering for the mistakes he himself had made in marrying Suzy. But despite the awful things she'd done, he couldn't hate the woman who'd borne him a son. But he sure as hell resented her. He'd been stupid to believe she'd ever loved him.

Thankfully, Josh's tears had stopped almost as abruptly as they'd started. Dan was glad, even though there was no possible way the ache in his heart would go away as easily.

Watching the light play across Molly's red-gold hair as she cuddled Josh close was only a partial distraction. He knew it was his fault that Josh was suffering right now. His fault that he'd been too distracted by Josh's mother, who'd called out of the blue after six years of absence, asking for money, to notice the car barreling through the intersection, straight toward them.

Even now, he could hear the screeching tires, the sickening *thunk* of metal crushing against metal. The agonizing sound of Josh's high-pitched scream.

He wanted to put his hands up to cover his ears, but that would be useless as he knew the noise would reverberate over and over in his mind, where nobody else could hear it but him. With a herculean effort he dragged himself out of the dark past to the just-barely-lighter present.

He couldn't ever make up for the injuries Josh had suffered that fateful night. All he could do was to try and start over. He'd taken a leave of absence from work so that he could rebuild his relationship with his son, at the same time doing whatever was necessary to ensure his son would walk again.

"Okay, Josh, we're going to sit back on the exam table here, so that I can massage your legs a bit before we use the ultrasound machine," Molly was saying now, lifting Josh up, despite her slim build, and setting him back on the table, as if Josh hadn't suffered a meltdown five minutes ago. "Do you know what an ultrasound machine is?"

Slowly Josh shook his head. "Will it hurt?" he asked.

Dan's heart squeezed in his chest. His son had suffered several surgeries to his injured legs, and every single one of them had hurt him.

He wanted to promise Josh that nothing would ever hurt him again. but obviously that wasn't exactly realistic.

"Not one bit," Molly assured him. "I'll show you how it feels on your hand. And we can try it on your dad first, so that you know I'm telling you the truth."

Dan roused himself to respond to Molly's unspoken demand. "I don't mind trying the ultrasound," he managed, even though he couldn't believe that Josh's first therapy session was almost over. In his mind Molly hadn't done nearly enough work with his son, and now the session was winding down. He silently vowed to get a few minutes alone with her to find out what sort of exercises he should be doing with Josh at home.

He stood, and helped Molly maneuver Josh into position so that she could massage his legs. Dan had to give her credit, Molly never once stared in horror at Josh's numerous surgical scars.

"Try to relax, Josh," she murmured, as she smoothed some sort of paste substance on her fingertips, before gently beginning to massage Josh's right leg. The leg that had taken the brunt of the crash. "Now, you let me know if I'm hurting you, okay?"

Josh nodded, and he grimaced a bit when she gently massaged the knot in his calf muscle.

"You have a very tense muscle right here," she said, using her thumb to smooth over the area. "I know it's a little sore, but you'll feel much better afterward if I work on it now."

"I know," Josh said bravely, and once again Dan's heart squeezed in his chest for what his young son was going through. If he could have taken the pain for Josh, he would have. But of course he'd walked away from the crash virtually unscathed.

And felt guilty about that part, too.

He tuned out a bit as Molly and Josh chatted about his school, as she asked him what his favorite subjects and teachers were. Since the crash, he'd hired a tutor to work with Josh so that he could keep up with his classes while he attended therapy every day.

But his ears pricked up when he heard his son talking about Mr. Iverson, the tutor he'd hired. "I don't like him. He's mean."

"What did you say?" he demanded, before Molly could respond. "What did Mr. Iverson do that was mean?"

Josh's lower lip trembled. "He yells at me. He makes me do adding and subtracting over and over again, even though I don't understand it. But he doesn't explain anything, just keeps making me fill out the worksheets and yelling at me when they're not right."

Dan frowned darkly. How was it that he hadn't known about the problems Josh was having with his teacher before now? "Well,

I'll get rid of Mr. Iverson. You should have told me sooner, Josh."

Instantly Josh's eyes brightened. "Really? No more math?"

"Now, Josh," Molly admonished gently, inserting herself into the conversation, "do you really think you can pass first grade to go on to second grade without learning to add and subtract?"

Josh gave a very adultlike sigh. "No, I suppose not."

"Sometimes school is hard, just like therapy," Molly said, moving over to massage Josh's other leg. "But there are things we can do to make them both fun."

Was he imagining it, or was that last comment directed squarely at him? He tried not to scowl but since when was school supposed to be fun? Kids had to learn, but tests, writing essays, memorizing history and practicing your sums wasn't exactly fun.

Was it?

"The muscles in your left leg aren't nearly as tied up in knots as those in your right leg," Molly said, turning the conversation back to the issue of therapy. "Do you feel the difference?"

Josh nodded vigorously. "Yep. Doesn't ache very much at all."

"I'm glad. Now we're going to use the ultrasound machine. Here's the wand, feel how smooth it is?" She picked up what looked like a stout hammer, except that the base of it was much wider and very smooth to the touch.

Josh tentatively put his hand over the end of the wand. "Yeah, it's very smooth."

"I'm going to move it in small circles over your skin, like this." Molly demonstrated again, on the palm of his hand. "Now, when I turn the machine on, it's going to make some noise and you'll feel a very faint vibration but it won't hurt. Do you want me to show you on your dad first?"

Josh nodded again, and watched with wide eyes as Dan extended his arm so that Molly could use the ultrasound machine on him.

She squirted cool gel on his arm, and then flipped the switch on the machine and moved the ball of the wand over his skin in a circular motion. He frowned. "I can barely feel the vibration. Are you sure it's turned on?"

"I'm sure. I told you this wouldn't hurt a bit." She glanced over at Josh with a bright smile. "Are you ready to try it?"

"I'm ready." Josh braced himself, and Dan

couldn't help moving closer to his son, putting his arms around Josh's thin shoulders. When she squirted the ultrasound gel on his skin, Josh jumped. "It's cold!"

"I know. And that's the worst of it, I promise." Molly pressed the ball of the ultrasound wand against Josh's leg and moved it in small circles.

Instantly Josh relaxed. "It really doesn't hurt!" he exclaimed in surprise.

"Josh, I will never lie to you," Molly said solemnly as she continued with the ultrasound therapy. "Remember when I told you the exercises were going to be hard to do? And they were, right? I will always be honest about what we're going to do, okay?"

Josh grinned. "Okay."

Dan waited patiently, as Molly finished up the ultrasound treatments, doing eight minutes on Josh's right leg and four minutes on his left. He didn't understand what good the treatments would be, though, as he honestly hadn't felt a thing when she'd practiced on his arm.

So far all they'd done had been to play several games, get a massage and then this weird, painless ultrasound therapy. Not that he wanted his son to be in pain, but surely there had to be more to therapy than what he'd seen today?

Was this Molly Shriver really the best in the business?

If so, maybe he needed to consider other alternatives.

Molly could tell that Dr. Morris wasn't thrilled with how Josh's therapy had gone today, and while she wished he'd trust in her knowledge and judgment, she figured that allowing anyone else to be in control went against the grain of a top-notch cardiothoracic surgeon.

And she still needed to talk to him about Josh's wheelchair.

"We're all finished, Josh," she said, scooting her chair back and putting the ultrasound machine away. She took out a towel to wipe the ultrasound goop from Josh's legs. "Now, I'm going to have you sit here for a few minutes while I talk to your dad, okay?"

"Okay."

"Heavens, I almost forgot!" She whirled round and picked up a candy jar full of lollipops. "Here, what's your favorite flavor? You get to pick any one you like for working so hard today."

She thought she heard a faint snort from Josh's father, an indication perhaps that he didn't think Josh had worked hard at all, but she ignored him. Josh debated the multitude of flavors. He took his time, as if this was the most important decision he'd make in his life, so she waited patiently until his fingers delved into the jar. "Grape," he announced, pulling out the lollipop with the purple wrapper. "I like grape."

"Grape is one of my favorite flavors, too," she confided, putting the lid back on the candy jar and setting it aside. "Now, wait here for a minute, okay?"

He was too busy sucking on his lollipop to answer. She gestured for Josh's dad to follow her out into her private office.

Once they were alone, she didn't beat around the bush. "I want you to get Josh a wheelchair." Dan, er—*Dr. Morris*—towered over her, topping her in height by a good eight inches. But she refused to be intimidated even though he was clearly angry.

"Josh isn't permanently handicapped," he said tersely. "He doesn't need a wheelchair. He's going to learn how to walk again. At least, he would if you were doing more than playing silly games."

The cutting edge of his tongue only made her square her shoulders to face him with renewed determination. "This isn't about what you want or need, Dr. Morris, it's about your son. It's about giving him the freedom to move around without waiting for you or someone else to carry him. It's about giving him independence. And lastly it's about strengthening his core muscles, his torso." She was growing angrier by the second.

"Don't you understand how important core body strength is when it comes to walking? You stand there and mock what I've done today, but those games I played with Josh were core-strengthening games. And therapy doesn't have to hurt in order to achieve results!"

He actually stared in shocked surprise at her outburst. A tiny voice in the back of her mind warned her to stop while she was ahead, but she was on a roll.

"Furthermore, how dare you question my methods? I have good outcomes, the best in the region. Do I stand over your shoulder and tell you how to operate on a damaged heart? This is my job, my career, and I'm damn good at it."

Her temper flared easily, she didn't have

red hair for nothing, but it dissolved as quickly as it ignited. She took several deep breaths, immediately feeling bad at how she'd lost control. Was she crazy? A powerful surgeon like Dr. Dan Morris could make or break her career.

Well, he probably couldn't totally break her career, as she really did have excellent outcomes that spoke for themselves. But he could make her life miserable.

And what if he stopped referring patients to her? The very idea made her gut clench and roll.

Why, oh, why hadn't she bitten her tongue?

The silence stretched interminably between them, until she decided he was waiting for an apology.

One he honestly deserved.

But before she could take her foot out of her mouth to formulate the words, he totally surprised her. "Where can I get a pediatric wheelchair?" he demanded.

"Um, right here. I can get you one from the storage room." She didn't move, though, afraid that he'd capitulated too easily. She licked her lips nervously. "Look, I'm—"

"If you wouldn't mind getting it now, I'd be happy to reimburse you for it," he interrupted, as if impatient to get the wheelchair now that he'd decided Josh really did, in fact, need one.

She nodded and quickly left the office to rummage around in the back storeroom. She found a perfect-sized wheelchair for Josh, and brought it back to his father.

He stared at it for a long moment, before dragging his gaze up to meet hers. "I never meant to take away Josh's independence," he murmured, his gaze full of stark agony. "That's the last thing I would ever want to do."

She felt her eyes prick with tears, hardly able to bear to see the lines of tortured self-reproach grooved in his cheeks. "I know. You were seeing the wheelchair as a sign of giving up. But encouraging Josh to use an assistive device isn't giving up at all. Trust me, this is just the first step on the road to Josh walking again."

His jaw tensed and his intense gaze seemed to drill all the way down to her soul. "Do you really believe that?" he asked hoarsely. "Do you really believe he'll walk again?"

"Yes." She couldn't stop herself from stepping closer and placing a reassuring hand on his forearm. The warmth of his skin shot tingles of awareness dancing along her nerves.

But she kept her gaze centered on his, ignoring her inappropriate reaction. "I believe he will. I won't lie to you, though. Josh's leg muscles are weak, so this isn't going to happen overnight. He has a long way to go. But I know he'll be able to walk again."

He covered her hand with his, surrounding her with even more heat. "I'm going to hold you to that," he said wearily.

She gave his arm a reassuring squeeze, and then subtly pulled out of his grip. "No more than I'm holding myself accountable," she assured him. They'd gotten past the first hurdle, but there would be more. She took a deep breath and let it out slowly. "You're going to have to help," she added. "Because Josh can't do this on his own. He'll need your support."

To her surprise, he nodded in agreement. "I know and that's perfectly fine with me. Obviously, he's not going to be able to walk with just one hour of therapy a day. I expect you to give me a list of leg-strengthening exercises to do with him at home."

She wanted to roll her eyes heavenward at his determination to direct the physiotherapy of his son. She supposed this tendency of his was part of being a surgeon but, really, hadn't they already gone through all this? She was the one in charge, here, not him.

The sooner he recognized that fact, the further along they'd be.

"Now that you mention it, I do have a list for you," she agreed as she headed over to her desk. She picked up the bright blue folder, and then came back over to hand it to him. "Inside you'll find everything you'll need. And, of course, I'll be seeing Josh five days a week. You've asked for early morning appointments, so he's scheduled every day at 9:00 a.m."

"No problem," he agreed readily, as he opened the folder to peek inside. He scanned the printed pages she'd tucked in the pockets, and then looked up at her with a deep frown. "These aren't exercises," he accused. "They're *games*." He emphasized the last word as if it was a curse.

She tried not to smile, but her mouth quirked up at the corners despite her best effort. "Yes, I'm aware of that, Dr. Morris. Your son is seven years old. Surely you know how to play games with him?"

She could have sworn there was a momentarily blank look in his eyes, before he snapped the folder shut with a flash of annoyance. "Of course I do."

This time she couldn't stop the smile from blossoming on her face. "Don't worry," she said, patting his arm as if he were one of her small patients, rather than a big, broad-shouldered heart surgeon. "You'll get better with practice."

CHAPTER THREE

MOLLY WAS PHYSICALLY exhausted by the time she finished her day, and while she'd cared for many patients during her nine-hour shift, it was young Josh and his enigmatic father who lingered in her mind as she took the subway home.

She tried to scan the newspaper she'd purchased at the hospital, as she normally did, but her mind kept wandering. She couldn't help wondering about how Josh was handling his new wheelchair, and whether or not Dr. Morris had unwound enough to play a few games with his son.

And she found herself hoping that the uptight surgeon wouldn't overdo things with Josh in his eagerness to get the boy walking again. If he pushed Josh too hard, the poor kid would be too sore to participate in her games tomorrow. Moderation was an important aspect of physical therapy and she realized now that she should have made a point of reinforcing that fact before they'd left.

She doubted Dr. Morris knew anything about moderation. The way he'd watched her, with his incredibly intense gaze, had made her feel extremely self-conscious. And far too aware of him.

Her cheeks burned as she remembered the way she'd let him have it in her office. Normally she didn't find it at all difficult to keep her temper under control, at least within a professional setting. But somehow Josh's father had pushed her buttons in a big way. The memory of her tirade made her wince. She'd have to make sure she kept her cool during their session tomorrow.

Would Dr. Morris bring his son in again? Or would he send Josh to someone else? Everyone knew that Dan Morris was single— there was a lot of talk about him being one of Angel's most eligible bachelors, especially now that Dr. Tyler Donaldson had been snagged by Dr. Eleanor Aston.

But whereas Tyler was a flirt, Dan was an enigma. Composed. Aloof. She didn't doubt for a moment that he had a nanny to help care for his son. The thought that she might not see Dr. Morris in the morning left her feeling curiously disappointed. That was crazy, because it wasn't as if she had any interest in the guy, other than how he needed to learn how to unbend enough to help his son.

She was so lost in her thoughts that she nearly missed her subway stop. At the last moment she grabbed her backpack and her newspaper and elbowed her way through the crowd to dash out the door seconds before they closed. Thankfully, the weather was mild for spring, so it was no hardship to walk the few blocks home to her tiny apartment.

Inside, she quickly heated up some leftovers and forced herself to finish reading the newspaper. She liked being up to date on current events, especially as the length of her commute didn't provide any time to watch the news.

When she opened the entertainment section, she stared in shock when she recognized her sister, Sally, and boyfriend, Mike, smiling together in a huge photo announcing their engagement.

Sally and Mike were engaged? Since when? And why hadn't anyone called her?

She couldn't seem to drag her gaze away from the beautiful, happy couple. Her sister was as dark as she herself was fair, making it even more noticeable that they weren't bonded by blood. Molly had been adopted by the Shrivers when she'd been four years old, but shortly thereafter her adoptive mother had discovered she was pregnant.

When Sally was born, Molly had been thrilled to have a younger sister to play with, but as they'd grown older, it had become clear that Sally, as the biological daughter, had been the favorite and she herself had too often been simply an afterthought.

Nothing had changed in the years since they'd both grown up. No matter how hard she tried to belong, when it came to her family, she remained the outsider, looking in.

Seeing her sister's engagement photo soured her appetite, so she shoved the newspaper aside and carried her dishes to the sink. She shouldn't be so upset at how Sally had gotten engaged without telling her, but she was. She knew her family hadn't done this to her on purpose, they weren't mean-spirited, it was more that they often forgot about her.

If she called her mother now to ask about Sally's engagement, Jenny would profusely apologize and offer some weak excuse to try to cover the fact that Molly hadn't been included.

For a moment, a deep sense of loneliness weighed down her shoulders like a heavy blanket. All she'd ever wanted was to be a part of a family. She'd thought her prayers had been answered when the Shrivers had adopted her, but over time she'd become less and less a true member of the family.

And since she'd graduated from college her one attempt to have a family of her own had backfired. James had been several years older than she was, a divorced father with two young boys. She'd met him when one of his boys had been injured playing soccer and she'd performed his therapy. They'd dated for five years, and she'd been sure he'd propose marriage, but instead he'd called off their relationship, claiming he'd fallen in love with someone else.

He'd broken her heart, although now, a year later, she could admit she'd loved his two young sons more than she'd loved him.

Not seeing James's boys anymore had left a huge, aching hole in her life. In her soul.

Her heart squeezed painfully in her chest. She didn't belong, not with the Shrivers and certainly not with James. On a professional level she belonged at Angel's, and working there had been the best decision of her life.

It was too bad that on a personal level it seemed she was destined to live her life alone.

Dan swallowed a curse as he wrestled to get Josh's wheelchair back into the trunk of his car. Josh didn't seem to like the stupid chair, despite Molly's insistence that having it would give him more independence. And Dan hadn't appreciated the sympathetic stares aimed at his son when they'd ridden down in the elevator together. One of the reasons he had balked at using the chair had been to save Josh from being teased about it.

Although maybe if he'd used the wheel-chair with Josh from the very beginning, his son would be that much further along with his therapy.

More to feel guilty about. As if everything Josh had been through, the prolonged hospi-tal stay and multiple surgeries, hadn't been enough. With an effort he shoved his dark thoughts aside.

"Ready, Josh?" he asked, as he slid behind the wheel.

"Yep." One good thing was that Josh hadn't been upset about going to therapy this morning. And he hadn't clung to Gemma, his nanny, begging her to take him. Dan knew part of the reason was that Josh was looking forward to seeing Molly again. However, he hoped there were also tentative bonds forming between him and his son.

Yesterday, when they'd gotten home, he'd fired the tutor who'd been mean to Josh and had called the school to arrange for a replacement. This time a young college freshman by the name of Mitch came to the house and Josh seemed to flourish under the kid's fun and somewhat laid-back approach.

As he'd watched them together, he couldn't help thinking Molly would approve.

After Josh's lessons they'd played the ball game again and the entire time Molly's parting words had played over and over in his mind. *Don't worry, you'll get better with practice.*

His gut still burned with the memory. He hadn't felt that inadequate since his internship year.

Despite being seriously annoyed with her, he had to admit to feeling some grudging admiration for Molly. No one had ever dared to stand up to him the way she had. And what was that she'd said? Something about how she wouldn't stand over his shoulder and tell him how to do heart surgery? Earlier in the session she'd called him Mr. Morris, but she'd obviously known who he was the whole time.

He supposed it was possible that she'd only figured it out after spending more time together. While he often referred patients to her, based on her reputation for being the best, it wasn't as if they'd worked together side by side. He simply wrote the order and then asked his patients and their parents how things were going when they came in for their routine follow-up visits. They'd always given him rave reviews about her care.

As far as his own opinion of her went, the jury was still out. She might be a pretty woman, with a bright, sunny attitude, but he wasn't going to be happy until Josh was walking again. And despite what she claimed, he had trouble believing these games of hers would really work.

The traffic was heavier this morning, and he drummed his fingers impatiently on the steering wheel as they waited for yet another red light. This time, when they arrived at Angel's physical therapy clinic, they only had five minutes to spare.

Five minutes that was taken up by wres-

tling once again with the stubborn wheelchair. Once he got the thing unfolded and
the footrests put back together, he lifted Josh
out of the car and placed him in the seat.

This time Molly was waiting for them
when they arrived. "Wow, you look awesome
in that wheelchair, Josh."

His son brightened under her admiration.
"Really? You think so?"

"Absolutely. And today we're going to
practice getting in and out of it, okay?"

"Okay."

"This way," Molly said, gesturing for them
to follow her into the large therapy room.
Dan pushed Josh's wheelchair forward. "If
you wouldn't mind stopping right there," she
said, when he reached the center of the room,
"I'd like to see what Josh can do on his own."

Letting go of the chair and backing off
to watch his son struggle to move the large
wheels forward was difficult. Josh's small
arms seemed far too skinny to be of much
use, although he did manage to wheel the
chair all the way over to Molly.

"Excellent." Once again she knelt before Josh so they were at the same eye level.
"I need you to practice wheeling yourself
around, Josh. I know your arms will get tired,

but you still need to practice. It's the only way to get your arms stronger, all right?"

"All right."

"Good." Molly's smile was bright enough to light up the whole room. For the first time Dan wondered just what her life was like to make her so happy all the time. He'd noticed that she wasn't wearing a wedding or engagement ring, but that didn't mean she wasn't seeing someone. He couldn't imagine a woman like Molly being without a man, so he had to assume she was involved. Why that thought made him feel depressed, he had no clue. The last thing he needed was a woman to further complicate his life.

After Suzy had upped and left six years ago, he'd vowed to never let a woman get close to him again. Josh needed stability in his life more than he himself needed female companionship. He'd willingly thrown himself into his career. Maybe a little too enthusiastically, now that he thought about it.

"I'm going to help you stand up, okay? First we have to set the brakes." She put her hands over his smaller ones to show him how to move the levers forward. "Now, I'm going to put my arms underneath yours, but I need you to push up on the arms of your wheelchair at the same time."

He watched Josh struggle to stand, noticing that Molly took a good portion of his weight in order for him to accomplish the task. Although once he was standing, she made him balance there for a few seconds.

"I'm going to fall," Josh whined. "Don't let me go or I'll fall!"

"I won't let you go, Josh, I promise," Molly assured him. "Just try and stand here for a little bit."

After another ten seconds she let him sit back down in the chair. Dan watched intently so that he could practice this at home with Josh.

"Good job," she praised his son. "Did you play any games with your dad last night?"

Josh nodded. "Yep, we played the ball game before dinner. It was fun. And I have a new tutor, too. His name is Mitch. I like him way better than Mr. Iverson." Josh screwed up his face in an apparent attempt to mimic the stern tutor.

Molly's lips twitched as she fought a smile, but when she lifted her gaze over Josh's head to meet his, Dan could see frank approval reflected in her gaze. And despite the fact he shouldn't care what she thought of him, he was secretly glad to have earned her favor.

The session went on, with more games that she dragged him into playing, and he was thrilled to notice that Josh was able to move his legs a little better today when Molly instructed him to kick the ball between his feet.

When she ended Josh's session with another massage and the ultrasound treatment, he couldn't help voicing his concern. "What exactly is the purpose of doing the ultrasound on his legs for eight minutes? I don't see what good it can possibly do for him."

She arched a brow, as she continued providing the treatment. "These are very intense ultrasound waves that are focused directly on the injured muscles. They help increase blood flow, which in turn helps to reduce pain and swelling," she said patiently, as if speaking to a first-year medical student.

"Really?" He frowned, trying to work through the pathophysiology of what she described. "And ultrasound waves are safe and harmless?"

"Definitely safe and harmless," she agreed. "But that doesn't mean they don't have helpful properties, as well. I also wanted to mention that you shouldn't let Josh overdo the games at home. What you did yesterday was perfect. An hour in the evening is enough so that Josh doesn't overwork his injured muscles. We wouldn't want him to suffer from muscle spasms."

He nodded, unwilling to admit how much he'd wanted to push Josh into playing her therapy games for longer than he had. Not because he wanted Josh to overwork his injured muscles but because he desperately wanted to see his son walk again.

Patience was a virtue, he reminded himself. Although having patience while performing heart surgery was far easier than having patience with his son struggling to learn how to stand and walk.

When she'd finished the ultrasound therapy, she handed Josh the candy jar, and this time it didn't take him long to choose a cherry-flavored lollipop. Dan figured that by the time they'd completed the initial twelve weeks of therapy, his son would have tried every flavor several times over.

"Okay, Josh, I'm going to talk to your dad again for a few minutes," Molly said as she put the candy jar away. "Wait here and I'll help you get into your wheelchair when I return."

Josh nodded, the skin around his lips already stained red from the cherry sucker.

Dan followed Molly's petite frame back to her office, trying not to imagine what her figure looked like beneath the baggy scrubs.

"Dr. Morris—" she began, but he quickly interrupted her.

"I asked you to call me Dan," he reminded. "I'll be attending therapy with Josh because I'm his father, not because I'm a surgeon here at Angel's."

"Ah, okay, Dan, then," she murmured. She paused, as if she'd lost her train of thought, and he took a moment to savor the way she'd said his name. For the first time in six years he preferred hearing his first name to his formal title.

"I want you to consider getting a wheelchair, too," she said.

He blinked, and tried to gather his scattered thoughts. "You mean one for Josh to use here as well as the one he'll use at home?"

"No, I mean one for you to use specially while we're working together with Josh." She tilted her chin in a gesture he already knew meant that this was a topic she felt strongly about. "Josh needs you to be a role model for him. And he needs to learn how to get in and out of it by himself. I think he would find that easier to do if you were learning alongside him."

Was she crazy? He'd never heard anything more ridiculous. What good would it do for him to be in a wheelchair, too? "I appreciate your advice but I don't see the need to get myself a wheelchair."

"Dr. Morris—Dan," she corrected swiftly, "You don't have the option to refuse. You have to stop questioning everything I do or suggest. Like the ultrasound treatments, and now getting a wheelchair of your own. For years you referred your pediatric patients to me, but now suddenly you're acting as if I have no clue what I'm doing. Why can't you believe I only have your son's best interests at heart?"

"I do believe that," he said slowly. He forced himself to meet her emerald-green gaze. "It's just…" He trailed off, unable to find the words to express how he felt. Because she was right. He was acting as if she didn't have a clue what she was doing. Just because he wasn't an expert in physical therapy, it didn't mean she wasn't. He had to trust her expertise and knowledge.

But getting a wheelchair of his own seemed

over the top. He wasn't the one who'd been injured.

Yet it was his fault that Josh had been.

He swallowed against the hard lump of the bitter truth. Did it matter if he felt stupid using a wheelchair? Wasn't Josh's recovery worth it?

"Look, we need to settle this now, before we go any further in treating Josh because if you can't or won't trust me, there's no point in us continuing."

Her last sentence made him scowl. "Are you threatening me?"

"It's not a threat. I'm only telling you that you either heed my advice and do what I say as it relates to Josh's therapy, or you find someone else to work with." She shrugged, as if she didn't care what he would decide to do. "I'm not the only therapist here, there are many others equally qualified."

He clenched his jaw, unable to believe she was actually handing him an ultimatum. He couldn't help it that it was his nature to question things. To make sure he understood what was going on.

"A good therapist-patient relationship is the key to success. Maybe I'm not the best fit for you," she said, when he didn't respond.

"But you are the best fit for my son." The moment he'd uttered the words, he knew they were true. Molly had a way with children, and it was obvious that Josh was already anxious to please her. Not to mention none of the other therapists had her amazing outcomes.

He'd tolerate whatever she decreed in order to help Josh. "I'll accept your terms," he said, roughly shoving his ego aside. "I'll get a wheelchair so Josh and I can learn how to use them together. And I promise not to question your methods from this point forward. I'll place my son's care in your capable hands."

She stared at him for a few seconds, as if struggling to see inside his mind, to believe he actually meant what he'd said. He didn't know what else to say, to help her understand how he'd meant every word seriously. Nothing was going to get in the way of Josh's ability to learn how to walk again.

Nothing!

If Molly Shriver had been hoping to get rid of him, she would be sorely disappointed. He was in this for the long haul. For Josh's sake.

No matter what.

CHAPTER FOUR

MOLLY WAS SECRETLY relieved that Josh's father hadn't decided to move his son's care to another therapist. Remembering how she'd issued her ultimatum made her cheeks burn with embarrassment. Once again she'd allowed her redhead temper to get the better of her. Why on earth did Dan Morris bring out the worst in her?

She took a deep breath and tried to prepare herself for their upcoming appointment. If she was smart, she would have insisted Josh be assigned to someone else. Emotionally, it would be better for her, as the young boy was already wiggling his way into her heart. And once he didn't need her anymore, he'd take a piece of her with him, leaving a tiny hole behind.

But somehow her instinct for self-preservation seemed to have abandoned her. Because it wasn't just Josh she was beginning to care about.

His stern-faced father was even more intriguing.

Watching the two of them navigating their wheelchairs in the gym had given her a deep sense of satisfaction. The proud and hopeful expression on Dan's face when Josh successfully transferred himself from the wheelchair to the therapy table and back again had been heartbreaking. It was clear how much he cared for his son. And she had to give Dan credit for keeping his promise. He hadn't questioned her or interfered in her treatment plan in the past two days.

Today was Friday, their last session before the weekend. She had a surprise for Josh, and hoped his father wouldn't revert back to his old ways. She'd learned as the week had progressed that Dan did better with structure rather than impulsiveness. Maybe that's what made him such a good cardiothoracic surgeon.

That was too bad. She worked better by following her instincts. And today her instinct was to get outside and have some fun. Especially on this unseasonably warm day in early March. Why stay inside when the temperature was in the fifties and the sun was shining?

When she was paged by the front desk to let her know that Josh and his father had arrived, she picked up her jacket and the red plastic ball before heading out to the waiting room to greet them.

"Good morning, Josh, Dan." Calling Josh's father by his first name was getting easier. In fact, he was looking less and less like the strait-laced cardiothoracic surgeon who'd shown up here four days ago. Especially dressed in his well-worn jeans and Yankee sweatshirt that only enhanced his broad shoulders.

"Hi, Molly," Josh greeted her enthusiastically from his wheelchair. "We're ready for therapy, right, Dad?"

"Right," Dan agreed with a rare smile. He looked surprisingly comfortable seated in the adult wheelchair alongside his son.

"I'm glad, especially as I have a surprise for both of you." She fought a smile as Dan immediately tensed up. Heaven forbid she plan a surprise. "We're going on a little field trip to Central Park!"

"We are?" Dan said with a frown. "That seems too far out of the way for an hour of therapy."

"The patient who was scheduled to see me after Josh cancelled so we have two hours free. Most of the snow has melted and as it's a beautiful day, we may as well enjoy the sunshine." She could tell he wasn't thrilled with the idea. "Come on, we'll have fun."

Dan opened his mouth as if to argue, but then closed it again without saying a word.

"Yippee!" Josh said with exuberance. "I love field trips!"

She grinned, relieved to see her patient was happy with the idea. And because Dan had promised not to question her motives, he couldn't very well disagree.

She walked alongside Josh as he wheeled his chair back down the hall toward the elevator. Dan followed in his own wheelchair right behind them, and while he didn't utter a single word of complaint, she could feel his displeasure radiating off him.

She sighed, hoping he wasn't regretting their bargain, because if he switched therapists now, Josh would certainly suffer.

Thankfully, Josh kept up a steady stream of chatter as they made their way outside. The sun was warm, but the air still held a hint of coolness as winter slowly gave way to spring, perfect weather for Josh and Dan, who'd be exerting themselves in order to use their wheelchairs.

The park was just a couple of blocks down from the hospital so it didn't take long to get there. The hardest part of the trip was navigating around the people crowding the sidewalks. Good ole New Yorkers, couldn't move over to give two people in wheelchairs room to maneuver.

They reached the south end of the park and followed the sidewalk inside. "Okay, Josh, you have to find us a good place to play ball," she instructed him.

"How about right over there?" he suggested a few minutes later, pointing to a relatively isolated grassy area.

"Perfect," she murmured. "Do you need help going over the grass?"

"I can do it," Josh said, his face intent as he exerted extra pressure to wheel himself over the bumpy terrain. Dan followed his son's example, even though he remained unusually quiet.

She plopped down on a park bench and tossed the ball up in the air, enjoying the sun on her face as she caught it again. "Remember the game we played that first day you came into the office?" she asked, directing her question to Josh.

"Yeah," Josh said, stopping his wheelchair not far from where she was seated. "Are we going to play catch again?"

"We are. But I want you and your dad to spread out a bit, so we're like the three points of a triangle."

Josh obediently moved his wheelchair back a foot. When she glanced over at Dan, he was doing the same thing.

"Excellent. Now, remember how we did it before, okay?" She tossed the ball high in the air toward Josh, who caught it easily.

"Good job, Josh," Dan said, breaking his silence.

Josh flushed with pleasure and turned his chair so that he was facing his father, before he tossed the ball up in the air. Dan had to lean over the side of the chair a bit to catch the ball, but he managed just fine. He tossed it back up in the air toward Josh.

"Molly!" Josh called, mere seconds before the ball landed on her head and then bounced off erratically. She laughed and jumped up to race after the ball.

"Caught you napping, didn't he?" Dan

drawled, a smile tugging at one corner of his mouth.

She grinned and nodded. "I can't tell a lie, he certainly did."

"Good thing you have a hard head," he teased.

"Good thing." Her smile widened. She could hardly believe he'd made a joke. "I bet yours is harder," she goaded as she quickly tossed the ball at him.

She'd used a little too much force, though, and the ball caught the wind, veering off to the left, out of his reach. But that didn't stop him from stretching up and over the side of the chair in a valiant attempt to reach it.

And suddenly the wheelchair tipped sideways, dumping him onto the ground.

"Dan!" she said.

At the same time Josh yelled, "Daddy!"

She rushed over to his side. "Oh, my gosh, are you all right?" she asked anxiously.

"Fine," he muttered, his cheeks stained red with embarrassment.

"Tell me where it hurts," she murmured, pulling the chair out of the way.

He groaned and rolled onto his back, staring up at her. "Mostly hit my shoulder, but I'm fine."

"Let me see." She leaned over him, running her fingers up his muscled arm to his shoulder. Thankfully there was no bump or obvious injury that she could feel. But when she looked down at him, their faces were so close she shivered from the intensity of his gaze.

Time hung suspended between them as he reached up and cupped her cheek with the palm of his hand. For a moment she completely forgot that Dan was a cardiothoracic surgeon. And a single father.

She leaned into his caress, catching her breath at the way his thumb slid across her cheek.

"Daddy!" Josh's cry broke the moment and she quickly pulled away from Dan, glancing up at his son.

"Don't worry, Josh, he's fine," she assured him, trying to calm her own racing heart.

What was wrong with her? What was she thinking? Getting close to her patient and, worse, to his father would be nothing more than a detour to disaster.

A path she couldn't afford to take.

Dan chided himself for thinking about what Molly would taste like if he dared to kiss her.

He must have fried a few brain cells in the

sun to even contemplate such a thing. But that moment she'd leaned over him, her expression so full of care and concern, had made him ache to touch her. To hold her.

To kiss her.

And the way she'd pressed her cheek into the palm of his hand made him think that the attraction wasn't one-sided. In fact, he'd noticed her eyes had darkened with the same desire that shimmered through him.

It had been so long since he'd felt anything remotely like it that he wondered if he'd dreamed up the flash of desire?

"Do you need help?" she asked, reaching down as if to help him up.

"I'll get there by myself," he said, more gruffly than he'd intended. She snatched her hand back and then moved closer to Josh. For a moment he sat on the ground, trying to figure out how he'd get back into the wheelchair if he truly couldn't use his legs.

He prided himself on getting to the gym whenever possible between surgeries, but to lever himself up off the ground using only his arm strength to get back into the dreaded wheelchair was more than he could manage.

Feeling like a wimp, he gave up the pretense. He rose to his feet and plopped back into his chair. Seeing Josh's concerned gaze made him feel even worse, because for a few minutes there he hadn't thought about Josh at all.

Just Molly. Pretty, cheerful, stubborn Molly.

"Hey, don't worry, Josh. I'm not hurt a bit." He wheeled himself closer to his son. "Make sure you don't make the same mistake I did, okay?"

"Okay." Josh's worried expression eased.

Dan risked a glance at Molly, and immediately felt bad when he noted the tiny frown puckering her brow. He hated knowing that he was the source of the frown. Especially when she was always so cheerful.

Just another reason for him to keep his distance. He wasn't ready to get involved in a relationship. Clearly, after what happened with Suzy he didn't even know how to function in a true relationship. He'd forever remember the accusations Suzy had hurled at him when she'd walked out. She'd called him cold and heartless, blaming him for everything that had gone wrong in their marriage.

Molly deserved better than someone like him.

He wasn't stupid enough to believe the failure was all his fault, but unfortunately he knew much of what she'd said was true. He did work long hours. His patients did often come first.

He hadn't always been there for her. For Josh. Especially in those first difficult months after Josh's birth. And later, once the lure of spending his money had worn off, she'd moved on to someone else.

Pushing the dark memories aside wasn't easy, but dwelling on the past wasn't going to help. He needed to focus on the present. On Josh.

He was relieved when the tenseness between him and Molly faded as the morning went on. They sat on the grass and played the game Molly called kick the ball, and he was encouraged by how well Josh was doing even after just four days of therapy.

Josh was able to move his legs from side to side, kicking the ball from one foot to the other, something that he hadn't been able to do earlier in the week. A huge accomplishment, one that he knew he owed to Molly and her unorthodox approach to therapy.

Just another reason he needed to maintain a professional relationship with Molly. He refused to give her a reason to switch Josh to another therapist.

His son needed Molly, far more than he did.

Watching Molly's slim figure as she chased after the ball made his gut clench with awareness. He couldn't remember the last time he'd been with a woman. Too long. Maybe that's why he'd overreacted to the pressure of her hands against his shoulder. Any woman would probably have inspired the same response.

When the next ball Josh sent in her direction bounced up and hit her on the nose, she laughed, and he couldn't help smiling at the light, musical sound.

Who was he kidding? He hadn't been this acutely aware of a woman since well before Josh had been born.

"I think we'll have to head back," Molly said with obvious regret as she set the red ball aside. "I have another patient scheduled at eleven."

"No-o-o," Josh wailed, his previous good humor vanishing in a flash. He pounded his fist on the padded arm of the wheelchair. "I don't wanna go."

Dan empathized with his son, feeling the same sense of regret at knowing their time together was over. The reminder that this had been nothing more than a job for Molly was like a cold slap to the face.

"We'll come back again soon, Josh," Molly said as she crossed over and put her arm around Josh's thin shoulders, giving him a reassuring hug. "We sure had fun today, didn't we?"

Josh buried his face into her side and nodded.

"We don't have to leave yet, Josh," Dan found himself saying. Molly swung toward him, her face registering surprise, and he hastily clarified, "I know you have other patients to see, but there's no reason we can't stay longer."

"Oh, no, of course not." Was he imagining the flash of disappointment in her eyes? He must have been because now she sounded downright happy. "Would you like that, Josh?" she asked with a smile. "Wouldn't it be great to stay here longer with your dad?"

His son clutched at Molly and shook his head, sending a spear of disappointment straight through his heart.

Molly looked surprised and upset by his son's response but the last thing he wanted or needed was her pity. "It's okay, Josh. I'm sure you're tired, so maybe it's just better if we head home. Mitch will be coming over after lunch anyway."

Josh still didn't respond, so Molly spoke up, filling the abrupt silence. "Sounds good, then. Let's go." Molly gently eased away from Josh and smiled, even though he could tell she was troubled. As they headed out of the park her pager went off.

"Are we late?" Dan asked, mindful of the fact that her next patient could already be there, waiting for her back at the hospital.

"No, it's not that," she said slowly. "Apparently my eleven o'clock patient cancelled, too."

He shouldn't have been relieved by the news but he was. "Do your patients cancel a lot?" he asked, perplexed. "I mean, two in a row seems a bit much."

She grimaced and nodded. "Actually, this happens more than you'd think. Especially on days like today, when it's nice out. Or on bad-weather days. Or days close to the holidays…" Her voice trailed off and she shrugged. "Hey, it's part of the business. Some people just don't think physical therapy is important. But the good news is that now we don't have to hurry back."

"Did you hear that, Josh? We can stay another hour."

The way Josh brightened at the news that they could stay longer only reinforced the fact that he wasn't feeling too tired after all.

Josh just hadn't wanted to stay without Molly.

And, heaven help him, he couldn't blame his son. Not when he felt exactly the same way.

Molly shouldn't deny the wave of relief she felt that she didn't have to return to the hospital just yet. Being outside was glorious, but she knew it was more than that.

Josh and Dan were getting to her. She knew they needed this time together just as much, if not more so, than Josh needed his physical therapy.

"Daddy, can we have hot dogs?" Josh asked excitedly, when a hot dog vendor pushed his cart into view. "I'm hungry!"

"Why not?" Dan said with a smile. "I'm hungry too."

"I'll race you over there," Josh challenged, wheeling himself quickly along the path.

"You're on," Dan shouted, taking off after his son.

Molly laughed when Josh reached the hot dog stand first and then raised his hands over his head in a gesture of victory when he beat his father. She suspected Dan had let him win, and couldn't deny the warm glow she felt seeing them interact together.

Not for the first time she wondered what had happened to Josh's mother. Not that it was any of her business but, still, she couldn't imagine a woman giving up her husband and her son.

Her entire family.

For a moment her smile dimmed, but just then Dan turned and called over to her. "Molly, are you up for a hot dog, too?"

"Sure," she agreed, striding over. She couldn't explain why, but she was suddenly ravenously hungry.

"My treat," Dan said gruffly, when she pulled money out of her pocket. She stared at him with indecision until he added, "Please? It's the least I can do."

"All right," she agreed, shoving the money back into her pocket. She took the hot dog and loaded it up with ketchup and mustard, before following Dan and Josh over to the closest picnic table.

As they enjoyed the impromptu meal, she

couldn't help noticing that the three of them looked just like any other family enjoying a day at the park.

But of course this wasn't a date. It was therapy.

No matter how much she wanted to pretend otherwise, Josh and Dan did not belong to her. They weren't her family.

She needed to remember that as soon as Josh was able, they'd both walk away.

CHAPTER FIVE

DAN PACED THE LENGTH of the kitchen while Josh ate cereal for breakfast. He felt at a loss as to what to do with himself now that he had so much time on his hands. He'd given Gemma the weekend off to visit her daughter and granddaughter, and now the hours stretched endlessly ahead of him. When was the last time he'd had a week off work? Or a weekend that wasn't filled with peewee football, birthday parties and soccer?

He felt bad that Josh couldn't take part in sports anymore, although he sincerely hoped his son would be able to join again next year. And he couldn't help feeling guilty that he'd been a little annoyed with the chore of driving his son around prior to the car accident.

Now he'd give anything to see his son running up and down the soccer field again.

He flexed his sore muscles, having already worked out in his weight room, trying to sweat thoughts of Molly from his system. It was ridiculous to lose sleep over a woman.

Not just any woman, he corrected himself grimly. His son's physical therapist, a woman who wore sunshine and happiness like a brightly colored dress.

A woman so different from him that they may as well be suspended in different solar systems.

The phone rang, and he welcomed the distraction, jumping to answer it. "Hello?"

"Dan, Marcus here. One of your patients, Carrie Allen, came into clinic with pneumonia. I just wanted you to know I started her on antibiotics again."

He frowned, thinking he should go in to see little Carrie for himself. "Did you admit her?"

"No, luckily her mother brought her in early, so I think she'll be all right. I'm going to see her again next week and if anything changes, I'll admit her to Angel's."

Dan rubbed the back of his neck, trying to relax. "Okay, great. Thanks for letting me know."

"Are you planning to attend Jack Carter's going-away party next Friday?" Marcus asked.

"Where is Carter going?"

"He resigned as Chief of General Pediatrics to work with Nina Wilson at her pro bono clinic."

"Really?" He felt like he'd been away from Angel's for months, instead of just a few weeks. "Our loss. I would like to attend the party. Where is it?"

"Eight o'clock at the Ritz Carlton. Nothing but the best for Jack."

Dan made a note of the date and time. "By the way, what do you know about Molly Shriver, the physical therapist?" he asked, trying, and failing, to sound casual. "Do you know if she's seeing anyone?"

"I don't know, but I think one of the nurses here is a friend of hers. Just a minute." Before Dan could stop him, he put Emily on the line, who cheerfully explained how Molly had broken up with some guy a little over a year ago.

Feeling like a fool, he thanked her for the information and quickly ended the call. He wasn't proud of himself for eliciting gossip about Molly, but he couldn't help feeling pleased that she wasn't seeing anyone at the moment.

"I'm finished, Daddy," Josh said, pushing away from the table. Before he could move over to help him, Josh had swung himself from the kitchen chair into the wheelchair.

He'd been amazed at how quickly Josh had adapted to using the wheelchair and had found getting from one place to another far harder than he'd ever imagined, giving him a new perspective for what his patients had to go through.

Heck, he'd even fallen out of the stupid contraption yesterday at the park. Although the minute Molly had come over to tend to him, embarrassment hadn't been his biggest concern. Instantly, he'd wanted nothing more than to kiss her.

An impulse that he thankfully hadn't acted on.

He needed to stop thinking about her, or he was going to drive himself crazy.

"What are we going to do, today, Daddy?" Josh asked.

Good question. How pathetic that he had no idea how to entertain his son. What did other parents do with their kids on the weekends? He had no clue. He racked his brains.

"We could try that new indoor game place," he offered. What was the name of it? Fun and

Games? "Even with your wheelchair, I think there are lots of things you can do."

"Really?" Josh's eyes lit up with excitement. "Can we ask Molly to come, too?"

It was on the tip of his tongue to refuse, except for the fact that he'd had the same idea. "I'll give her a call, but I don't know if she'll agree to come," he cautioned Josh. The last thing Dan wanted was to get his son's hopes up. "She might already have plans for today."

Or she might refuse, simply because going with them was crossing the line of professionalism.

His hands were damp as he dialed her number. She didn't answer so he left a message, giving his phone number and asking her to call him back if she was interested in going to Fun and Games with him and Josh. When he hung up the phone, he had the depressing thought that she might not bother to return his call.

He hid his disappointment when he turned back to his son. "Sorry, champ, but Molly wasn't home. I left her a message, but I think we're on our own today. But we'll have a great time anyway, right?"

"Right," Josh agreed without enthusiasm.

Dan wished there was something he could

do or say to cheer him up. But it was hard to be upbeat when he felt the same way.

He was worse than Josh, counting the hours until Monday when they'd see Molly again.

Molly listened to the voice-mail message at least three times, secretly thrilled at hearing Dan's husky voice inviting her to go along with them to Fun and Games. She'd managed to push him from her mind during her three-mile run, but now he was back there, front and center.

Although it wasn't as if he'd invited her out on a date or anything, as Josh would be with them. And the indoor games place was hardly a romantic setting but even so, she was tempted, oh, so tempted to say yes.

She tried to rationalize her desire to go, telling herself this little outing could be just an extension of Josh's therapy. Josh had already made great progress in just five days—surely he'd be even further along if she helped him today?

Before she could talk herself out of it, she dialed Dan's phone number. He picked it up on the first ring and for a moment she couldn't speak.

"Hello?" he asked again. "Is this Molly?"

"Ah, yes, this is Molly," she blurted out, finally finding her voice. "I'm, um, returning your phone call." Brilliant conversation, she told herself, rolling her eyes. Just brilliant. Could she sound like a bigger dope?

"Molly, I'm so glad you called back. Would you be willing to go to Fun and Games with me and Josh? We'd love you to."

The eagerness in his tone soothed her frayed nerves. "Sure, what time?"

"Well, I thought we'd go later this afternoon and then stay for dinner, although they mostly serve pizzas and burgers. With the traffic in New York, I could pick you up at two or two-thirty. If that's all right with you." Was it her imagination or did Dan sound nervous? "We could also play more of your games before heading out, if you think that would be all right."

"No, of course I wouldn't mind. Two o'clock sounds fine. Would you rather I meet you at the clinic? That way you don't have to drive all the way out here to the Bronx."

"Josh and I will pick you up, right, Josh?"

She had to grin when she heard Josh yelling "Yeah!" in the background.

"All right, I'll see you around two." She was about to hang up when Dan asked for her address. Feeling a little embarrassed, she rattled off the number of her apartment building. She knew it wasn't exactly in the best neighborhood, but it was all she could afford on her therapist's salary.

"See you soon," Dan murmured huskily.

"All right," she managed, before hanging up. For a moment she couldn't move, stunned by what she'd just agreed to. Was she crazy? Didn't she have any self-preservation left after James had dumped her last year?

Apparently not, since she didn't make a move to cancel her plans. No matter how stupid, she was looking forward to seeing Dan and Josh again.

She usually cleaned on Saturdays, and as she had a few hours to kill, she stuck to her routine. When she'd finished, she showered and dried her hair, deciding to keep her hair down rather than pulling it back into a ponytail, the way she usually wore it at work.

This wasn't a date, but she still managed to try on just about every article of casual clothing that she owned, which admittedly wasn't much. She wore scrubs to work and didn't have enough money to be a clotheshorse. In the end, she settled on a pair of well-worn jeans and a bright green short-sleeved shirt that brought out the color of her eyes. Perfect attire for Fun and Games, although she wished she had something to wear that would make her look nice for Dan.

Stop it, she lectured herself. She was going along to help Josh with his therapy. Nothing more.

And maybe if she repeated that several more times, she'd find a way to believe it.

When her apartment buzzer went off at five minutes before two, she quickly crossed over to answer it. "I'll be right down," she said through the intercom, not wanting Dan to see her sparse furnishings. She'd gotten most of them from a secondhand store, and nothing matched.

She was surprised when only Dan was there, waiting for her in the minuscule lobby. "Where's Josh?" she asked.

"He's in the car, I'm double-parked outside," Dan admitted with a wry grin. "Let's go before I get a ticket."

She laughed and shook her head. "They wouldn't dare give Dr. Daniel Morris, renowned pediatric cardiothoracic surgeon at Angel's, a ticket."

He didn't say anything in response, but when he put his hand in the small of her back, gently urging her forward, she felt his light touch all the way down to her toes.

Get a grip, she told herself sternly.

Thankfully, Josh was excited to see her, diverting her attention from the ridiculous attraction she felt for his father. "Hi, Molly!"

"Hi, Josh. How are you feeling?"

"Good. Are we gonna play some more games today?" he asked. "I have more fun with you."

She winced at Josh's blunt statement and glanced over at Dan, noticing his mouth was set in a grim line. She knew he cared deeply about his son, and it couldn't be easy for him to hear Josh express his feelings.

No wonder Dan had asked her to come along today.

"Sure, we'll play some more games," she agreed, covering the awkward silence.

She was relieved that Josh kept up a steady stream of chatter as Dan drove back to their place. When they arrived, she waited patiently for him to pull Josh's wheelchair out of the trunk of the car, before heading to the elevator. She wasn't the least bit surprised to see that Dan lived in a luxurious apartment on the top floor, one that no doubt cost twenty times her annual salary. She tried not to feel intimidated as Dan showed her to the playroom.

"Where are you going?" she asked, when he turned to leave. "You have to play with us, right, Josh?"

"Right," Josh agreed.

She thought Dan's smile dimmed a bit, although he stayed in the playroom with them. Determined to make the most of the time they had, she ran them through a series of games, which had Josh giggling with enjoyment by the time they were through.

"Enough," Dan cried, throwing his hands in the air. "I give up!"

"What do you think, Josh?" she asked. "Should we let your dad off the hook?"

"No," Josh said, shaking his head. "Let's beat him again!"

She felt bad for ganging up with Josh against his father. "No, that's not fair. This time I think you and your dad should go against me."

"Actually, I don't think we have time," Dan said gently. "We have to get going, if you want to eat dinner any time soon."

She glanced guiltily at her watch, realizing they'd played far longer than planned. "All right, then, let's go."

Technically, after the time she had just spent with them, there was no need for her to really go to Fun and Games with them. For a moment, it crossed her mind to beg off. She could easily take the subway home.

But she held her tongue as Dan helped Josh put on jeans and a T-shirt. "Look, Molly, we match!" Josh said excitedly, pointing to his green shirt.

"So we do," she murmured, knowing that she didn't have the heart to disappoint Josh by backing out of their plans now.

Not even to save herself from more heartache.

"I'm hungry, Daddy," Josh complained as he drove to Fun and Games.

He glanced at his son, in the rearview mirror. "I know. We'll be there soon, okay?"

"Okay," Josh agreed.

"I'm hungry too, Josh," Molly said, swiveling in her seat so she could face him. "What are you going to have? Pizza? Or a burger?"

"Pizza!" Josh shouted.

Dan smiled, but kept quiet as Molly chatted with Josh. When he'd first picked her up at her rundown apartment building, he'd almost turned round and left. The fact that Molly didn't have a lot of money made him wonder, just for a brief moment, if she was looking for a rich husband, the way Suzy had been. But it wasn't fair to compare her to Suzy, so he thrust the thought aside.

And when she'd come down to the lobby, a bright smile on her face, he'd nearly swallowed his tongue. She was stunning, even wearing simple figure-hugging jeans and a bright green blouse. He appreciated the curves that had previously been hidden by her baggy scrubs. And she'd left her red-gold hair down, gently framing her heart-shaped face, leaving him to wonder if the strands would feel as silky soft as they looked.

Did she have any idea the effect she had on him? How distracted he'd been by her the entire time they'd played therapy games with Josh? He'd hardly been able to tear his gaze off her long enough to catch the ball. He didn't even care that they'd ganged up on him, not when the sound of their laughter rang through his home.

He couldn't remember the last time Josh had laughed so much. Too long, he decided. Far too long.

And he had Molly to thank for it.

He pulled into the jammed parking lot, realizing that many other parents must have had the same idea to bring their kids here to play. Normally, he'd avoid these types of places like the plague, yet for some reason, tonight he was looking forward to it.

Something else he could thank Molly for.

He pulled out Josh's wheelchair, and quickly unfolded it. He'd become an expert over the past few days.

"Wow," Molly murmured in awe, when they took the ramp into the building. There were games lining all the walls, a bouncy house in the middle of the room and of course plenty of picnic table type seating. "This is amazing!"

"It's loud, that's for sure," Dan mumbled with a sigh. He had to smile at the way Molly glanced around in awe, as if she'd never been inside a place like this.

"What do you want to play first?" she asked Josh.

"I want to hit the gophers!"

He grimaced and led his son and Molly over to the video game where several gophers popped out of holes and the goal was to bop them on the head to push them back in. The player scored a point for every gopher they hit.

Molly giggled as Josh started smacking the gophers. "Get 'em, Josh, get 'em!"

"Are you hungry?" Dan asked, once Josh had finished his game. "There's an empty table right over there."

Molly nodded, and quickly crossed over to the table. He was impressed at how well Josh managed to finagle his way through the games room with his wheelchair.

"What will you have?" he asked.

"Well, Josh wants pizza, so that would be fine with me," she admitted.

"No problem. I'll put in our order." He felt a little guilty that the only food he'd provided for her so far had been fast food, but when the pizza arrived, she and Josh both dove into the meal with such relish that he suspected she didn't mind. Besides, there was no point in wishing he could take her to a nice restaurant, where they could enjoy a quiet meal by candlelight.

This evening was for Josh. Not for him.

He discovered Molly was a kid at heart and she threw herself into the games with gusto. She also had a highly competitive streak, getting frustrated when he beat her score on the gopher game. And when she finally topped his score, she jumped up, whooping as loudly as his son.

"I think you've lost your voice," he said, when they made their way back out to the car some hours later.

"I know," she said hoarsely, with a tired smile. "But it was worth it."

He gave her credit for thinking that, since his ears were still ringing from the bells and whistles shrieking from the various games.

Josh yawned widely, trying to keep his eyes open. "That was so fun, Molly. I'm glad you came with us."

"Me, too," she whispered.

Dan watched his son in the rearview mirror, smiling to himself at how hard Josh fought to stay awake on the way home. But they'd only been in the car for fifteen minutes when his head dropped off to the side and he fell asleep.

Now that he was essentially alone with Molly, he found he couldn't come up with a safe topic of conversation.

"You're doing a good job with Josh," she said hoarsely, breaking the silence. "How is it that you're able to come to all his therapy appointments?"

"I took a leave of absence from work," he

admitted. "And it's well worth it because he's responding so well to therapy."

"Yes. He is."

He was tempted to reach over to take her small hand in his when suddenly Josh cried out. "Ow, Daddy, it hurts. It hurts!"

"What's wrong, Josh?" Instantly, Molly twisted in her seat, reaching back for Josh. "What hurts? Tell me what hurts?"

"My legs," he cried. "Make it stop! They hurt so bad!"

"What's going on, Molly?" Dan asked, keeping his attention on the road. He'd been about to head for Molly's apartment to drop her off, but they were closer to his place, which was only five minutes away.

"I think he's having muscle cramps," Molly said, with a worried expression on her face. She quickly unbuckled her seat belt and managed to climb into the backseat. "I'll work on massaging his legs, but it would work better if he was lying down."

"We'll be home in less than five minutes," he told her.

Dan could hear Molly trying to talk soothingly to Josh as she worked on his legs, but his son was still crying out in pain.

"Mommy!" Josh cried, sobbing as he arched his back in the booster seat. "I want my mommy!"

Helpless fury banded Dan's lungs, making it difficult to breathe. He gripped the steering wheel tightly, listening in agony to his son's suffering, as he pushed the car as fast as he dared to get Josh home.

CHAPTER SIX

MOLLY DID HER BEST TO massage the cramping from Josh's legs, knowing that it was her fault the child was in pain. She wouldn't blame Dan for switching therapists after this. She barely registered the fact that they'd arrived back at Dan's until he opened the door of the backseat and reached for Josh.

She unsnapped the belt holding Josh in. Wordlessly, his features tense, Dan scooped Josh from the booster seat and into his arms before striding toward the elevator, leaving her to scramble along behind them. Thankfully the elevator arrived quickly and she continued to massage the muscles in Josh's legs as they rode up to the thirty-second floor.

"His room is this way," Dan said gruffly, as he swung through the condo to Josh's bedroom. The boy had ceased screaming for his mother, but he was still crying. Each gulping sob broke her heart.

"I need some lotion," she said to Dan when he'd gently set Josh down. She climbed up onto Josh's bed in order to have a better angle that would enable her to use more pressure on his leg muscles. Dan returned quickly with a small tube of hand lotion.

She ignored the fatigue in her own fingers as she worked over Josh's legs. After about twenty minutes he stopped crying, but she still continued to massage his legs until she only felt the smoothness of relaxed muscles beneath the angry red scars.

She nearly jumped when she felt Dan's hand on her shoulder. "He's asleep, Molly. I think you can stop now."

With a brief nod she awkwardly tried to climb off Josh's bed, wincing as the muscles in her back cramped painfully from being bent over for so long. When she managed to get back on the floor, she stumbled and would have fallen if not for Dan's strong arms wrapping around her waist, holding her up.

For a moment she could only lean against him, reveling in the strength of his arms surrounding her as she breathed in his unique musky scent.

After a long moment she forced herself to break away, standing up on her own two feet.

She avoided Dan's gaze as she made her way back to the main living area. She dropped onto the sofa and mentally braced herself as she slowly raised her gaze to meet his, fully expecting to feel the scathing edge of his tongue.

"Thank you," he murmured. He sat down heavily beside her, scrubbing his hand over his jaw. "I don't know what I would have done if you hadn't been there."

She blinked in surprise at his gratitude. "It's my fault, Dan," she said, unable to take credit for helping Josh through the crisis when it had been her fault from the beginning. "I shouldn't have allowed him to overdo things this afternoon. I should have realized that he'd be moving around a lot with all the games."

"Josh was enjoying himself," he pointed out with a tired sigh. "If anyone is to blame, it's me."

She shook her head, knowing he was shouldering blame that wasn't his. She was glad Josh had fallen asleep and prayed that the muscle cramps wouldn't return.

When Dan didn't say anything for several long seconds she remembered how Josh had called out for his mother. She had to assume that Dan had joint custody of his son, but surely the boy needed his mother at times like this? "Are you planning to call Josh's mother?"

Instantly, his expression turned grim. "No."

She was shocked at his blunt refusal. How could he turn his back on his son like that? "Why not?" she pressed, refusing to listen to the tiny voice in the back of her mind telling her to mind her own business. "Josh was calling for her. He obviously needs his mother."

Dan muttered something that sounded like a curse under this breath as he rose to his feet. "Despite what you heard, Josh hasn't seen his mother in six years."

She sucked in a harsh breath, wondering if she'd heard him correctly. He'd raised Josh since he was a one-year-old? "Six years? Really?"

He rubbed the back of his neck. "Besides, my ex wouldn't come, even if I did call her," he finally admitted. "Not unless I offered her money. And I refuse to pay her another dime to be a mother to her son."

She opened her mouth and then closed it again, unable to think of anything to say in response. She found it impossible to imagine what had caused Dan's ex to turn her back on her husband and her son. "Her loss," she finally managed.

Dan's tense facial features relaxed. "I think so, too," he agreed softly. Then he cleared his throat and glanced toward his son's room. "Look, Molly, it's late and I know you probably want to get home, but I would rather you stayed here in case Josh's muscle cramps return."

His request caught her completely off guard. "Here?" she squeaked.

"In the guest room," he hastily clarified, ramming his hands into the front pockets of his jeans, looking distinctly uncomfortable. "It's the room right next to Josh's."

She didn't have any of her things, not even a toothbrush or a comb, but the thought of Josh's muscle cramps returning was enough that she couldn't bring herself to refuse. Staying to ease the child's pain was the least she could do. "Of course I'll stay."

Relief flooded his features. "Thank you. I have spare toiletries and will leave them in the bathroom you'll share with Josh."

She wanted to smile at the way he'd made a point of letting her know she wouldn't have to worry about stumbling across him in the middle of the night. She assumed that his master suite had its own bathroom. Not that she should even imagine him in his master suite. She quickly pulled her thoughts away from the image that bloomed in her mind. "Um, great! Sounds good."

"This way," he said, gesturing to the doorway of the spare bedroom with one hand.

She rose to her feet and followed him across the living room to the guest room. He paused next to her, so close she could feel the heat radiating off his skin.

"Thanks again, Molly," he murmured, staring down at her intently.

For a moment she thought he was going to kiss her, but instead he simply took her hand and squeezed it gently. She was glad it was dark, so he wouldn't see how she blushed. "You're welcome," she murmured, forcing herself to tug her hand gently from his when all she really wanted to do was to throw herself into his arms.

When he finally left, she leaned against the door and took several deep breaths, trying to calm her racing heart.

She needed to remember that he'd only asked her to stay for his son's sake, not because he wanted to be alone with her or anything. If she hadn't been able to hold on to

James, there was really no way in the world she had a chance with someone like Dan. He was way, way out of her league.

She brushed her teeth and vowed to take the subway home first thing in the morning, putting their relationship back on a professional level.

Where it belonged.

Dan didn't sleep very well, and while he'd have liked to blame his son's leg cramps, he knew the real reason was because Molly was just down the hall in the guest room.

So close.

Too close.

He finally crawled out of his bed at five-thirty, knowing that trying to sleep any longer was useless. And there was a tiny part of him that looked forward to seeing Molly this morning.

After a quick shower, he padded softly to the kitchen and peered inside the fridge. He wanted to make a nice big breakfast as a way to thank Molly for helping Josh through his crisis and staying last night.

He hadn't heard Josh wake up at all, and since he'd been awake half the night, he could only assume his son had slept peacefully.

After brewing a pot of coffee, he began pulling out the ingredients for French toast, Josh's favorite. He prepared the egg mixture so that he'd have things ready to go when Molly and Josh woke up. His stomach rumbled with hunger so he decided to cook thick slabs of bacon, as well.

"Do your patients know you eat like that?"

He spun round to find Molly hovering in the doorway, dressed in the clothing she'd worn the day before, only this time she'd pulled her long red-gold hair back into its usual ponytail, a style that made her look incredibly young.

Or maybe he was just incredibly old.

"Ah, good morning, Molly." What was it about her that made it difficult for him to think straight? He glanced down at the bacon with a guilty flush. "My patients are children, not adults. And, besides, having bacon once in a while isn't too bad, right?"

She laughed softly and hitched her purse over her shoulder. "I guess not, although I must confess I would have imagined you making wholegrain pancakes or granola and yogurt for breakfast."

He grimaced wryly. "Guess I've tarnished

my image, huh? Come in, have a seat. Would you care for coffee?"

She gazed longingly toward the coffee-pot, but slowly shook her head. "No, I should probably head home. I just wanted to thank you for your hospitality."

"You can't leave without eating breakfast," he said in a rush of panic, ridiculously upset that she intended to leave so early. "Did you really think I was cooking all of this for me?" he asked, gesturing to the meal in progress incredulously.

"Well…" she said doubtfully. "I don't want to impose on your family time."

He didn't have the heart to admit that he and Josh didn't exactly have family time, at least not in the way she probably thought. They had more of a trying-to-rekindle-their-broken-relationship-time, which consisted of awkward silences more than anything else.

"If you leave now, you would be impos-ing on me and Josh to eat all this food by ourselves," he teased, trying to keep his tone light. "Please sit down, and are you sure you wouldn't like a cup of coffee?"

She chewed her lower lip nervously, but then ventured farther into the kitchen, taking a seat on the stool in front of the breakfast nook. "I'd love some coffee. The mere scent was enough to wake me up from a sound sleep."

He busied himself with pouring her a mug of coffee, sliding it over to her before getting one for himself. "Cream, sugar?" he asked.

"Cream or milk, if you have some." She cupped her hands around the mug as if needing the warmth.

He brought out the milk, and then frowned. "Are you cold? I'll turn up the heat."

"Maybe a little," she admitted, rubbing her hands up and down her arms. "It's been so nice the past few days, but now I can see frost outside."

"Welcome to spring in New York," he muttered. "Hang on a minute, I'll get you a sweatshirt."

He flipped the bacon strips before he retreated to his bedroom, looking for one of his sweatshirts. He brought it out for her, oddly pleased at how she looked wearing his clothing.

"Thank you."

"It's the least I can do," he responded. "I, uh, hope you like French toast," he said, crossing back over to the stove. "It's Josh's favorite."

"I love it," she assured him. She took a sip of her coffee and he couldn't help thinking how pretty she was. Suzy had worn enough makeup to paint a clown, but he preferred Molly's fresh-scrubbed beauty any day of the week.

Forcing his gaze to the task at hand, he dunked the bread slices in the egg mixture and set them into the sizzling fry pan.

"Dan, I have a question for you and I hope you don't think I'm intruding or anything."

He glanced up from the French toast. "You can ask me anything, Molly," he said truthfully. After baring his soul to her last night about Josh's mother, he couldn't imagine what could be too intrusive.

"It's, uh, about Josh's birthday." She was staring down at her coffee as if afraid to look him in the eye. "I was wondering if you'd made any plans?"

He tightened his jaw, and spent a few minutes flipping the bread slices before answering. "No, I haven't planned anything yet," he said slowly. "But I'm guessing you think I should have some sort of party?"

"I don't want to tell you what to do," she said hesitantly. "But if you were going to have a party, I'd offer to help."

"You would?" He glanced up and caught her gaze. She looked so hopeful he found he couldn't deny her anything. "What sort of party are you imagining?" he asked with a mock frown.

"Here's what I've been thinking," she said, leaning forward eagerly. "We could get a whole bunch of wheelchairs from the clinic and invite Josh's friends to a game of wheelchair football. That way he could play with them, and I think his friends would get a kick out of it, too. We could serve either hot dogs and hamburgers or pizza for dinner. What do you think?"

He had to admit she'd nailed the best idea he'd ever heard. "I think it's a perfect idea. If the weather co-operates."

"I know. March is dicey," she murmured. "But as long as it's not snowing, they can bundle up and we don't have to play for hours. If it's cold, we can start at the park and then come here afterward." She glanced around at his immaculate apartment and frowned. "If you don't mind the fact that the kids will likely make a mess," she added doubtfully.

Normally, he wasn't ashamed at the fact that he liked his life neat and orderly, but the way she looked at his things made him feel slightly embarrassed. Since when was having a clean home more important than his son's happiness?

"I don't mind at all," he quickly interjected. "All that matters is that Josh and his friends have fun."

She relaxed, a bright smile blooming on her face. His gut tightened with awareness. He'd never been more attracted to a woman than he was to Molly. She was a beacon of light in his otherwise drab existence. "Great. There's no time to lose. We have to invite his friends as soon as possible."

"I'll call his teacher, I'm sure she'll give me the names of the kids in his classroom."

"You should invite all of them, girls, too," Molly informed him.

"Girls?" He didn't try to hide his surprise. "Really? Isn't first grade a little young for having girls over?"

"It's just the polite thing to do," she said. "Besides, we're planning this at the last minute, so I'm worried a lot of the kids might not be able to come."

He scowled as he scooped the slices of French toast off the griddle and stacked them on a plate. He hoped the kids in Josh's class would come, and hoped that giving them all wheelchairs to use would keep the teasing down to a minimum.

"Breakfast is ready," he said, carrying the plate over to the breakfast nook. He pulled the bacon out of the pan, too, blotting the grease and then stacking them on another plate. Lastly he pulled out the maple syrup, before sliding into the seat beside her, so close their elbows bumped.

He watched with amusement as she doused her French toast with enough maple syrup to float a boat. She took a big bite and then closed her eyes, as if savoring the flavor. "Mmm, absolutely delicious," she announced.

"Thanks." He took a bite of his food, admitting that it was pretty darned good. But he knew the main reason he was enjoying his meal so much was because of Molly. Somehow she had the ability to brighten his day with nothing more than a smile.

Selfishly, because he didn't have much to offer her in return, he found himself wishing that she would be around to share breakfast with him every morning.

Molly told herself at least ten times to leave Dan's to return home, but somehow she ended up spending the entire morning with him. And Josh.

She was thrilled that he'd agreed to her idea for Josh's birthday party. And if she was a little annoyed that he hadn't come up with something for himself, she put those feelings aside.

She was beginning to realize that Dan needed help, not just in learning how to play games but in learning how to be a father. What his ex had done, leaving him alone with a small son to raise on his own, was appalling. And while she understood he had a very demanding career, operating on young infants and children, surely they weren't more important to him than his son?

She couldn't help wondering about him, especially his past, even as she insisted on helping to clean up the breakfast dishes. To her surprise, Dan refused to let her do the work alone. Working side by side with him in such a mundane task as washing dishes brought a strange sort of intimacy to their relationship.

"I'd like to massage Josh's legs one more time before I go," she said as she finished drying the last pan. "Too bad I don't have the ultrasound machine here for him. He could really benefit from that therapy, too."

Dan scowled as he took the damp dishtowel from her. "I could buy one, if you think that would help."

"Buy one?" she echoed, aghast. "Do you have any idea how expensive they are?"

"Doesn't matter," he said with a shrug. "I'll buy one today, if you think it would help."

She could hardly believe he was really offering to purchase an expensive piece of equipment for Josh to use for such a short time.

But then again, wasn't she surrounded by luxury? Dan Morris obviously could afford an ultrasound machine. Or anything else he or Josh desired.

"Don't be ridiculous," she muttered. "We can stop by the clinic and use the ultrasound there just as easily."

"Great. And then maybe we can take in a movie this afternoon, too."

"Yeah!" Josh said with barely repressed enthusiasm. "Come on, Molly. Please? Please come see a movie with us?"

She wanted to say no. Needed desperately to put distance between them. Maybe Dan cooked breakfast like a normal person, but he was a pediatric cardiothoracic surgeon, for heaven's sake. Wasn't this fancy condo proof of how he moved in much higher circles than she could even fathom? She'd heard rumors that his salary was seven figures. Talk about a mind-boggling amount. She didn't make a tenth of what he did.

This…friendship, or camaraderie or whatever they had couldn't go anywhere. Why was she setting herself up for more heartache? She was destined to remain an outsider, and nothing was going to change that. Dan only thought he needed her now, but as soon as he'd repaired his relationship with his son, he'd move on.

"Please, Molly?" Josh said again. And looking down at Josh's big brown eyes, mirror images of his father's, she couldn't bring herself to say no.

"Yes, Josh, I'd love to see a movie with you."

CHAPTER SEVEN

GOING INTO THE physical therapy clinic on Sunday, when no one was around, felt strange. Molly didn't think she would get into trouble or anything but, still, she knew she'd be glad when she'd finished the ultrasound treatments to Josh's legs.

While she worked on Josh, she did her best to ignore Dan's intense gaze, but it wasn't easy. At this point she didn't think he was watching her because he didn't believe in her technique.

No, this time she had the distinct impression he was watching her out of some sort of personal interest. Not a romantic interest, she told herself quickly, but more as if she were some sort of alien creature that he couldn't quite figure out.

Maybe because she was so different from his ex? Hearing Josh cry for his mother had really bothered her. She couldn't imagine how Dan managed to cope with the demands of being a single parent.

"Can we go to the movie now?" Josh asked eagerly, after choosing a root-beer-flavored lollipop. She hid a smile, figuring he was planning to try every single flavor in the jar before starting over with grape.

"Sure thing, champ," Dan said with a gentle smile. Was it her imagination or was he already getting closer to his son? "We have plenty of time to get there before the show starts, no problem."

"Yay," Josh said, using his arms to propel his wheelchair forward as they made their way back out to the car. "I can't wait."

Dan sent Molly a wry smile over Josh's head. He'd already explained that Josh wanted to see the latest Disney film, and she honestly didn't mind. The last cartoon film she'd seen had been one that she'd watched with James's two sons.

And if she remembered correctly, James had begged off, claiming he had work to do. Now she wondered if he'd been seeing that other woman even then.

No reason to torture herself over that now. Her friend Kara had told her she was much better off without James, and while that had been difficult to believe at first, it was easier now. Today was about Josh, not her. She was determined to enjoy herself, while protecting her heart.

Getting to the movie theater didn't take long and once Dan had spent a small fortune on popcorn and soft drinks, they found a place in the back where Josh could sit in his wheelchair at the end of an aisle.

"Sit next to me, Molly. Sit next to me!"

She did as Josh asked, hoping Dan wouldn't mind. He didn't say anything, simply took the seat to her right, the action causing their shoulders to brush lightly. She settled back in her seat, telling herself to focus on the ultra-wide screen.

Flanked on either side by the Morris men made it difficult for her to concentrate on the movie. As the one in the middle she was the one stuck holding the bucket of popcorn. She grew acutely aware of Dan leaning over to help himself, especially when his arm stayed pressed against hers. Warmth radiated from his skin, sending shivers of awareness rippling along her arm.

But she didn't move away, despite knowing she should.

The movie was a cute story and she soon found herself giggling right along with Josh. And when she heard Dan laughing softly, she was secretly thrilled he'd unbent enough to enjoy the show.

"That was fun. Thanks for bringing me along," she said after the movie ended.

"I'll drive you home," Dan offered quickly. "Unless Josh and I could convince you to stay for dinner?"

"I couldn't eat a thing after all that popcorn," she protested. "Besides, I really need to get home."

"I understand," he murmured, although she caught a glimpse of disappointment shadowing his gaze.

Her resolve almost wavered. Almost. But she'd already let this go on long enough. What was she thinking, spending time with Dan and Josh as if they were more than friends? The last thing she needed was to make the same mistake with Dan and Josh as she had with James.

The ride to her apartment didn't take long. When Dan pulled up, he jumped out before she could stop him, coming over to open her door for her.

"Bye, Josh, see you tomorrow," she said as

she climbed out of the car. When Dan drew her toward him so he could close the door, she had the insane thought he was going to haul her into his arms and kiss her, but then he whispered in her ear, "I'll call you later to finalize the details about Josh's party."

She flushed and ducked her head, hoping he wouldn't notice her embarrassment. "Okay, sounds good." With a final wave to Josh she turned and hurried inside.

Feeling Dan's gaze boring into her back with every step.

Dan forced himself to get back into the car with Josh, when every cell in his body wanted to follow Molly. He was getting tied up in knots over the woman, and he knew it. Yet knowing it and stopping himself from thinking about her were two entirely different things.

Molly had helped him mend his relationship with Josh, but what he was feeling for her went beyond gratitude. He knew he needed to rein in his feelings, and fast.

But despite his firm pep talk, when he and Josh returned home he couldn't help noticing that the spacious three-bedroom apartment seemed empty now that Molly was gone.

Which was ridiculous. How was it possible that his home seemed complete only when Molly was here? Nothing made any sense anymore.

He turned on some music, hoping to fill the emptiness. He busied himself making arrangements for Josh's birthday party and the wheelchair football game. There wasn't much he could do on a Sunday night, but he vowed to contact Josh's teacher first thing in the morning. The party would take place in two weeks on Saturday afternoon.

So in the interim he made plans and lists, realizing that planning a party was a lot of work. And tried not to count the hours until Josh's therapy session at nine o'clock next morning.

The following morning, Dan called Josh's teacher first thing, and she was more than happy to help him give him a list of the student's names. She also offered to pass out the invitations in class, which meant he needed to get them completed as soon as possible.

He and Josh arrived for therapy in their respective wheelchairs with scarcely a minute to spare. As usual, Molly came out to greet them. She smiled warmly at Josh, but he sensed she was avoiding eye contact with him. He scowled as he wheeled into the gym behind them, wondering if she was uncomfortable around him now, after they'd spent the weekend together. If so, he couldn't understand why. He hadn't acted inappropriately at any time, although he couldn't say the same for his thoughts.

In his thoughts, he'd been extremely inappropriate. Down and dirty inappropriate.

"We're going to play a new game today. Are you ready?" Molly asked.

"Yeah!" Josh agreed enthusiastically.

"Absolutely," Dan responded, hating to admit that he was growing used to her games.

The game consisted of hitting the ball with their feet, which of course was much easier for him than it was for Josh. But he had to give his son credit, as he seemed determined to kick the ball up in the air with his toes.

He was shocked and stunned when Molly deemed it time for the massage followed by the ultrasound treatments. How had the hour gone by that fast?

When she'd finished with Josh's ultrasound, Dan quickly followed her out of the room, leaving Josh to enjoy his lime-flavored lollipop. "Josh's teacher has emailed me the names of the kids in his class, so I'm going to work on the invitations tonight."

"That's great!" For what seemed to be the first time that morning, she looked him directly in the eye and smiled. "Josh is going to be so surprised."

Her enthusiasm was contagious. "Here's what I have planned so far," he said. "We'll meet at the park first for the wheelchair football game, and then afterward we'll eat pizza, punch, cake and ice cream either at the park if it's nice or at my place if it's not."

"That sounds perfect," she agreed. "Don't forget prizes."

"Prizes?" He stared, perplexed. "I wasn't thinking of playing any other games."

"You need to reconsider that plan. What about a scavenger hunt?"

"A scavenger hunt?" Hell, hosting a party was more complicated than he'd realized. "I don't think I want the kids going around to the other apartments, asking for things." He couldn't remember the last time he'd participated in a scavenger hunt.

"We could have a scavenger hunt at the park, after the football game." Her green eyes brightened with excitement. "I'll hide a bunch of stuff at wheelchair height or lower, and they can try to find the items I've hidden. Whatever they find are their prizes. Although you'll need to make sure there's a prize for everyone."

He suppressed a sigh. More rules. More things to buy. He needed another list. "Okay, that'll work."

"We won't know what the weather will be like, so we might need a back-up plan. Maybe check again with Josh's teacher to see if the school would let us use the gym," she suggested. But then she glanced at her watch. "Sorry, but I have to go. My next patient is here."

"Okay, no problem." He took a step back, trying to hide a flash of disappointment. Not that he could blame her for needing to do her job. "See you tomorrow."

"Absolutely. Goodbye." Was it his imagination or was she in a hurry to get away from him?

As he went back to where Josh was waiting, he couldn't deny he felt a little lost without the connection he'd thought he had with Molly. Had he become too dependent on her?

The realization brought him up short. He couldn't afford to be too dependent on anyone.

Josh's happiness was the most important thing in his life, and he needed to remember that.

Granted, he appreciated Molly's help, but he was making strides in mending his relationship with Josh. He might be new at this hosting-a-birthday-party thing, but he was determined to be a good father. He wanted—*needed*—to make sure his son knew just how much he loved him.

Molly did her best to keep her distance from Dan, but it wasn't easy. On Tuesday night she called her friend Kara.

"Molly, it's so good to hear from you!" Kara gushed.

"I know, it's been too long, hasn't it? How are you holding up?"

"I'm doing okay." Kara's crush on Tyler Donaldson hadn't been much of a secret. However, now that the handsome Texas-born neonatologist had gotten involved with Eleanor Aston, Kara had been trying to mend her bruised heart. Especially now the two were head over heels in love and rumored to be expecting a baby. "I can't be mad at the guy, not when he's obviously so happy."

"Don't worry, you'll find someone just as perfect someday," Molly said stoutly.

"Actually, I have met someone," Kara said. "But we're just friends."

"Really?" She injected warmth into her tone, refusing to be envious of her best friend. "Anyone I know?"

"His name is David Jacobson and he's a new pediatric neonatologist at Angel's." Since Kara worked in the brand-new neonatal unit, she probably interacted with the new doctor a lot. "But we're just friends."

"Hey, you can't ever have too many friends," Molly pointed out.

"I know, and I value your friendship every day," Kara said. "By the way, would you be willing to go to Jack Carter's going-away party with me this Friday night? Did you hear he's having it at the Ritz?"

"No, I hadn't heard about the party, although I did hear that he handed in his resignation." Normally, Molly avoided fancy places like the Ritz, but maybe attending Dr. Carter's going-away party would be a good distraction. "What about your new friend, is he going to be there, too?"

"Yes, he's going and, yes, I wouldn't mind bumping into him there. Come on, Molly, please? I don't want to walk into this party all alone."

Molly knew Kara wanted a good reason to attend the same party David was going to, and since she knew Kara needed to get over Tyler, she couldn't say no. Especially as her own social life was practically non-existent. It wouldn't hurt her to get out and mingle more. "Sure. Why not? I'd love to."

"Thank you," Kara murmured. "It starts at eight o'clock and you have to wear something fancy."

She grimaced. "Oh, boy, that means I have to go shopping."

"And when was the last time you bought yourself something nice?" Kara demanded.

Since never. She'd worn a simple black skirt and green blouse for the ribbon-cutting ceremony, unwilling to spend her hard-earned money on fancy clothes. But it wasn't every day that the chief of pediatrics stepped down to work at a free clinic with his fiancée, so she swallowed her protest. "Okay, okay. I'll shop. Maybe I'll find something on sale."

"Did you hear who's been appointed Chief of General Pediatrics in Jack's place?" Kara asked.

"Who?"

"Dr. Layla Woods. I think it's awesome

that a female physician was given such a prestigious position, don't you?"

"Yes, it's great." Molly didn't know Layla Woods personally, although everyone talked about the tiny blonde bombshell and her sweet Texas accent. Not to mention her brilliance as a pediatrician. "She deserves the position."

"I agree."

"Are you sure you're okay?" she asked, when Kara went quiet. "I'm sure it's not easy to see Eleanor and Tyler together all the time."

"It was hard at first, but now they just seem so natural together that I can't help but be happy for them."

"You're amazing, Kara, you know that?"

"Thanks, Molly, so are you. Hey, look, I have to run, my break is over. We'll talk more later, okay?" Kara quickly disconnected the call and Molly could just imagine her friend running back to the unit to take care of her tiny patients.

Molly was glad Kara wasn't too heartbroken over Tyler and Eleanor's newfound love. She didn't want to be full of envy, but she hoped Eleanor knew how lucky she was. If the rumors were true about her and Tyler having a baby, a family, was the greatest gift in the world.

Images of Dan and Josh flitted into her mind, but she shoved them aside ruthlessly. The two of them were not meant for her.

Maybe Kara was right. Maybe she needed to get out more. Socialize. Meet people. Meet men. Someone other than a single father with emotional baggage from his horrible ex-wife. What if she became involved with Dan and he ended up leaving her, just like James had?

Walking into the living room, she turned on her laptop computer and logged into her bank accounts.

She needed to know how much she could afford to spend on a dress. Because maybe, just maybe, she'd meet someone at the going-away party who would help her forget about Dr. Daniel Morris and his adorable son, Josh.

The following morning, Molly did her best to keep Josh and Dan at a professional distance. Josh's therapy was coming along very nicely, and when she played the kick-my-hand game, she was thrilled at how high Josh was able to kick.

"Oomph," she grunted, playing it up a bit as she staggered backward, gazing at Josh in awe. "You nearly knocked me over!"

"I know," Josh said with exuberance. "I'm getting stronger, right, Molly?"

"You are definitely getting stronger, champ," Dan said, a wide smile on his face. "I'm so proud of you."

Despite her best efforts to stay detached from the dynamic father and son duo, her heart ached at the love shining from Dan's eyes. Her throat tightened, and for a moment she couldn't breathe.

"We have a lot to thank Molly for, don't we?" Dan said to Josh.

The boy nodded. "Yep. We love Molly, don't we, Dad?"

She couldn't talk, could barely think as Dan's gaze clung to hers. "Yes, we do," he agreed lightly.

She knew he didn't really mean it. At least, not in the guy-girl type of way. But she knew she was blushing just the same. "Enough, you two, we have more work to do before this session is over."

In truth, they only had one more game to play before it was time for the massage and the ultrasound treatment. She finished the therapy and handed Josh the jar of lollipops, watching with amusement as he chose a lemon-flavored sucker.

"Molly, do you have a minute?" Dan asked, as she was about to leave.

She glanced at the clock. "Just a minute. I have another patient waiting."

"I understand."

She walked down the hall to her office, all too aware of Dan following close behind. "Is there a problem? Has Josh been having more muscle spasms?"

"No, there's nothing wrong." Was it her imagination or did he look nervous? "I just wanted to know if you were busy on Friday night?"

For a moment she couldn't hear anything but her heart thudding in her chest. Was he really asking her out on a date? Then she realized he probably wanted her to spend time with him and Josh again. She sensed he liked having her as a buffer when he interacted with his son. Although they were clearly getting along better so she knew he didn't really need her.

"I'm sorry, but I already have plans. Maybe another time?"

The disappointment in his eyes tugged at her heart, but she did her best to ignore it. "Sure. Another time, then."

She tore her gaze away and glanced again

at the clock. Of course today every one of her patients was going to show up for their appointments. "I'll see you and Josh tomorrow, okay?" Without waiting for him to say anything, she quickly left her office, heading to the waiting room to greet her next patient.

Unfortunately, Dan's invitation looped over and over like a stuck tape playing through her mind as her day progressed. Along with the distinct disappointment in his dark eyes, when she'd told him she already had plans.

How pathetic to realize that deep down she would rather spend time with Dan and Josh, instead of dressing up for some fancy going-away party at the Ritz Carlton Hotel. If not for agreeing to Kara's plans first, she might have backed out.

What in the world was wrong with her, anyway?

CHAPTER EIGHT

AFTER MOLLY SHOT DOWN his invitation before he could even ask her to go with him,
Dan wasn't exactly looking forward to Jack
Carter's going-away party, but as the event
would be doubling as a fund-raiser for Nina's
pro bono clinic, he told himself that it was all
for a good cause.

Molly seemed to be back to her friendly
self by Friday, and it had taken everything
he had not to ask her out again, this time for
Saturday night.

He sensed there was more holding her back
than just the fact that he was the father of her
young patient. Molly was bright and cheerful most of the time, but there were the occasional moments when she seemed a little
sad. He thought about what his partner had
said, about Molly breaking up with her boyfriend about a year ago, and found himself

wondering what had happened. Had she broken things off? Or was she still in love with the loser?

The very thought of her being in love with someone else made him feel sick to his stomach. By all rights he should want Molly to be happy, yet somehow he only wanted her to be happy with him.

And Josh.

He donned his tux, which he'd had to dig out of the back of his closet, eyeing himself critically in the mirror. He'd asked Gemma to stay overnight in order to watch Josh, something he hadn't needed her to do since he'd taken his leave of absence from the hospital. Normally, Gemma only stayed overnight on the weeknights and weekends he was on call.

Luckily, she hadn't said anything about the fact that he was spending the time going out rather than working.

"Don't go, Daddy," Josh whined. "Stay home with me."

He paused in the act of drawing on his jacket. This was the first time Josh had ever asked him to stay home. The first time his son had indicated he might prefer his father's company over that of his nanny.

"I love you, Josh," he said, coming over to

crouch down next to Josh's wheelchair. "More than anything in the whole wide world."

"I love you, too, Daddy." Josh leaned against him, burying his face in his father's chest.

Dan kissed the top of his son's head, his heart swelling with emotion. He considered calling off his plans. It wasn't as if anyone would really miss him if he didn't show up.

"How about I stay here until it's time for you to go to sleep?" he said, trying to compromise. "We can read another book."

"Really?" Josh visibly brightened. "That would be awesome."

"Really." He followed as his son wheeled himself into his bedroom. He knew the party would start without him. And he'd only be a little late.

His son was far more important. Seeing the progress Josh was making helped ease his guilt for having been distracted the night of the crash. He was beginning to believe Josh really would walk again.

Now, for the first time in a long time, he had his priorities straight.

Molly paid the taxi fare and then walked into the Ritz Carlton Hotel. For several long moments she stood in the opulent lobby, gazing at the impressive high-domed ceilings and ornate white woodwork trimmed with gold as she waited for Kara to arrive. She smoothed a hand down her slinky green dress, and smiled as a couple walked by, wondering for the tenth time if the gown was too revealing. Not that it was extremely low cut or anything, but the way the fabric clung to every curve didn't leave much to the imagination.

She took a deep breath and let it out slowly, glancing down at her watch. It was barely eight o'clock, so it wasn't as if Kara was late. But she couldn't help feeling conspicuous, standing here alone.

A tall, handsome man with jet-black hair walked into the lobby, talking on his phone. "Hi, Callie, how is life in the great Down Under?"

Molly recognized him as Alex Rodriguez, one of the top neurosurgeons on staff at Angels. She turned away, trying not to eavesdrop on his conversation, although he wasn't exactly trying to be quiet. She noticed several other heads had turned in his direction, as well.

"I'm glad you're doing better, because I'm not," he said curtly. "Can you believe Layla

Woods has been appointed as the new chief of Pediatrics? Seems no matter how hard I try to move on with my life, that woman keeps popping back into it."

Molly moved a few steps away, even though Dr. Rodriguez had certainly captured her attention. Apparently not everyone was thrilled to have a female in charge of the pediatric division. Was there some personal history between him and Layla? She didn't often pay attention to the hospital grapevine.

"Don't get involved?" Alex let out a harsh, humorless laugh. "Yeah, thanks for the warning, Callie. You and I are way too much alike, so I'll say the same right back at you."

There was another pause as he listened to something Callie said. "Thanks for the invite, but I'm not running away. Especially not from a woman."

Just as Alex Rodriguez finished his call, Kara walked in, looking very glamorous in a midnight-blue dress that displayed her slim figure to full advantage. Molly quickly crossed over to greet her. "Wow, Kara, you look amazing!"

Kara laughed and hugged her. "So do you, Molly."

"Maybe, but I think a certain doctor is

going to be shocked when he catches a glimpse of you," she teased.

"From your lips to his ears," Kara said with a laugh. "And if he doesn't notice me, hopefully someone else will. So, are you ready to head up there?"

Molly took a deep breath and nodded, telling herself she needed to mirror Kara's attitude. "I'm ready if you are."

They took the grand curving staircase up to the main ballroom. A waiter greeted them at the doorway, holding a tray of drinks. Molly and Kara both helped themselves to glasses of sparkling champagne.

"This is the life," Kara murmured. "I see David is here, over by the bar."

"Maybe you should wander over?" she suggested.

"Maybe in a bit," Kara said. "This place is amazing, isn't it?"

"Absolutely." Sipping her champagne, Molly gazed out over the audience, quickly verifying that Dan wasn't among the mingling crowd. Not that she'd expected him to be here. She knew he was likely to be at home, spending time with Josh.

"I've heard Jack normally doesn't flaunt his wealth, but he and Nina are using this party as a way to collect donations for her pro bono clinic," Kara continued, filling her in on the latest gossip.

"I'd be happy to donate," Molly murmured. She'd gotten the emerald-green floor-length gown at a steeply reduced price, so she had a little extra money to spare.

"Let's go say hello to the guest of honor," Kara murmured, drawing Molly toward the large group gathered in the center of the ball-room. Kara was far more outgoing than she was, and she often wished she had the same confidence.

After signing the pledge card to donate funds for the clinic, she smiled and chat-ted with the other guests, feeling a little like a fraud. This wasn't the type of place she normally hung out at. No, she was far more at home eating pizza at places like Fun and Games.

She caught sight of a familiar dark-haired woman in the crowd and stopped dead in her tracks. Sally? Was that really her sister, Sally, standing there with her fiancé?

Before she could turn away, Sally glanced over and saw her. There was momentary confu-sion on her face before recognition dawned. Instantly, Sally took her fiancé's arm and dragged him over to where Molly was standing.

"Molly! What a surprise to see you here!" Her sister gave her a quick hug before turning toward her fiancé. "Mike, you remember my sister, Molly, don't you?"

"Of course. How are you, Molly?" Mike asked.

She forced a smile to her face, trying not to point out that the last time they'd talked had been three months ago, at Christmas. "I'm fine, doing great. Busy at work as usual."

"Yeah, Sally's been busy at work, too," Mike said. She wasn't surprised, as Sally worked on the orthopedic floor as a nurse. "Angel's is always hopping, that's for sure."

"Molly, guess what?" Sally gushed. "Mike and I are officially engaged!"

She didn't let on that she'd already seen the engagement notice in the paper. "Really? Oh, Sally, that's wonderful. I'm so happy for both of you."

"Thanks." Sally held out her hand, and Molly oohed and ahhed over the sparkling diamond.

"He totally surprised me, didn't you, Mike?" Sally said with a laugh. "Not that I'm complaining or anything."

"Aw, that's so sweet. Congratulations to both of you," Molly said, meaning every word. Even though they hadn't included her when they'd first gotten engaged, she was truly thrilled for them. Her sister deserved to be happy.

"Thanks, Molly. We had the best Valentine's Day ever, didn't we, darling?" Sally linked her arm with Mike's. "Oh, look, there's Aaron Carmichael. Come on, Mike, I'll introduce you. See you later, Molly," her sister tossed over her shoulder, before dragging her intended away.

For a long moment Molly couldn't move. Couldn't breathe. Valentine's Day? Sally and Mike had gotten engaged on Valentine's Day? Almost a month ago?

And no one had called her? Not even her parents?

Tears burned her eyes and she spun round and hurried out of the ballroom, intending to seek privacy in the ladies' room. But in her hurry to escape she plowed into a broad chest. "Excuse me," she murmured, trying to pull away.

But strong hands gripped her shoulders. "Molly? What is it? What's wrong?"

Belatedly, she recognized Dan's voice and

his familiar musky scent. In some part of her mind she was surprised he was there, but at the same time she was too upset to wonder about that. And when he wrapped his arms around her, holding her close, she closed her eyes against the tears and rested her forehead against his chest.

"Shh, it's okay. Whatever happened, I'm sure it will be okay," he murmured.

She wished she believed him, but she knew firsthand there was no way to make someone love you. To care about you. She was so steeped in her misery she barely noticed when he led her away to a small private alcove out of range from prying eyes.

Dan had nearly swallowed his tongue when he'd entered the ballroom of the Ritz Carlton and seen Molly dressed in a figure-hugging emerald-green dress, revealing curves he'd only dreamed about.

But then he'd realized she was crying and he'd immediately scowled, searching for the person who'd upset her. He figured it was the guy who'd broken things off with her last year.

The jerk.

Although he was glad the jerk was a jerk

because otherwise she wouldn't be available. Just then she'd barreled into his chest and he'd caught her close, more than willing to hold her in his arms.

Although he wished she was here for some other reason than the fact that she was struggling not to cry. After Suzy, he'd avoided women's tears like the plague. After all, his ex had turned them on and off at will, using them like a weapon.

But Molly's tears were different. For one thing, she was hiding them from him, as if she was embarrassed. And for another he could feel her body tense, deep breaths shuddering through her as she struggled to get herself back in control.

"I'm sorry I got your tux wet," she whispered, pulling away and sniffling loudly. She brushed her hand over his suit, as if to wipe away the evidence of her tears.

"I couldn't care less about the tux, Molly," he chided softly. He used his thumbs to wipe the dampness from her cheeks. "I hate seeing you so upset."

She tried to smile, although he didn't have the heart to tell her it was a pathetic attempt at best. She straightened and glanced around.

"Where's the bathroom? I need to fix my face."

There was nothing wrong with her face that he could see. "Molly, you look beautiful, as always. But if you really need to go into the ladies' room, it's across the hallway."

"Thanks." This time her smile was genuine as she touched his arm lightly. "I'll be back in a few minutes, okay?"

"I'm not going anywhere," he promised before she hurried away.

And he didn't move, not even an inch, until he saw her emerge from the bathroom a few minutes later. As before, she took his breath away, only now she was truly radiant as she smiled and nodded at a couple walking past.

His mouth went dry as she approached and he was glad to see that all evidence of her brief crying jag had vanished from her face. Except for the hint of sadness shadowing her eyes.

"I lost my glass of champagne," she announced. "How about we go in and find one of those cute waiters carrying trays filled with glasses?"

He chuckled and took her hand in his so they could stroll back into the ballroom side by side. "Far be it for me to stand in the way of you and a glass of champagne."

They found a waiter without too much trouble and Dan picked up two glasses, handing one to Molly. "Here you go. Did you come alone tonight?" He was proud of his casual tone.

Molly took a big gulp of champagne and shook her head. "No, I met up with my friend Kara Holmes. She's here, someplace."

He frowned, trying to place the name. "Does she work at Angel's, too?"

"Yes, she's a nurse in the neonatal unit. She's over by the bar, talking to one of the new doctors on staff." Molly took another sip of her champagne, catching his gaze over the rim of her glass. "Do you mind if I ask you a question?"

He raised his eyebrows. "Of course not."

"When you asked me if I had plans on Friday night…" She hesitated, then said, "Were you planning to come here all along?"

For some odd reason he wanted to grin. "Yes, I was planning to ask you to come with me tonight. And you shot me down before I even had a chance to ask." When her expression fell, he hastened to reassure her. "But none of that matters as we're both here now."

He was glad, very glad he hadn't canceled out at the last minute.

"Yes, we are."

Molly drained her champagne and was looking around for another waiter, so he quickly reached for her hand. "Come on, let's dance."

The band was playing a slow number, and he was grateful for the excuse to pull Molly back into his arms. She was several inches shorter than he was, even with her heels, yet somehow she managed to fit into his arms perfectly.

"Wow, you're a great dancer," Molly murmured, tipping her head back to look up at him.

It took every ounce of willpower not to lower his mouth to kiss her. He tried to remind himself that she deserved someone better than him, someone who knew how to laugh and love, but logic flew out the window when she gazed up at him like that.

As if she cared not about his money but about him. As a person, not a meal ticket.

He cleared his throat and tugged her close. "You're a great dancer, too."

When the song ended, she moved away and

he reluctantly followed her over to the side of the room.

"Molly!" A dark-haired woman came rushing over. "Introduce us to your...*friend*."

He sensed Molly stiffen beside him, but her smile didn't waver. "Oh, sure. Sally and Mike, this is Dan Morris, one of the cardiothoracic surgeons at Angel's. Dan, this is my sister, Sally Shriver, and her fiancé, Mike Drake."

He made sure that none of his surprise that this woman was Sally's sister showed on his face as he slid a casual arm around Molly's waist. "Pleased to meet you."

"Aren't you going to ask why we don't look anything like sisters?" Sally demanded with a slight slur to her voice. She staggered a bit and he sensed she'd already had several glasses of champagne.

"Hey, Sally, watch out there. Are you okay?" Mike stepped in to steady his fiancée. "Come on, honey, I think you need to eat something."

"Good idea," Dan murmured. "Molly, let's dance again before we eat, okay?"

She acted as if she hadn't heard him, and she didn't say anything when Mike eased Sally toward the buffet table set up along the far side of the wall. She stared after them for several long moments, before blurting out, "The Shrivers adopted me when I was four years old."

That explained the difference in their looks, but why did she seem so upset by that fact?

"Molly, look at me." He waited until she turned to face him. "I don't like the way your sister managed to upset you. Was she the reason you were crying earlier?" When she nodded, he was glad to know she hadn't been pining over her last boyfriend.

"I didn't know you were adopted, but it's not the end of the world, is it? Do you think something like that matters to me? I don't understand why you look like you just lost your best friend. Do you think being adopted is something to be ashamed of?"

"No, I'm not ashamed," she said slowly, her gaze thoughtful. "But it just occurred to me that maybe Sally is."

"If so, that's her problem, not yours." Dan tried to keep the edge of anger out of his tone. "Besides, why would you listen to her when she's half-drunk?"

"You're right, she's not herself. Although I guess I always hoped we'd be close friends." Molly sighed and shook her head before she glanced up at him. "Never mind my sister. If you meant what you said a few minutes ago, I'd love to dance."

As if he needed to be asked twice. "My pleasure."

He escorted her onto the dance floor and pulled her into his arms. This time, instead of keeping a proper distance between them, she cuddled close, slipping her hand up and around his neck.

His pulse tripled as she pressed against him, her unique fragrance filling his head. For several long moments he could barely think, probably because all the blood in his body had headed south. But he wasn't dreaming. Molly was really here with him. Because she wanted to be. Not because she was drunk, as he was pretty sure she'd only had the one glass of champagne. After seeing her sister staggering after her fiancé toward the buffet, she seemed to have lost her taste for bubbly.

He smoothed his hand down her back, thinking he would be content to spend the rest of the night like this. Dancing with Molly.

Holding her.

Kissing her.

When she lifted up her head to look at him,

he wondered if she had the ability to read his
thoughts because she rose up on tiptoe and
pressed her sweet mouth against his.

CHAPTER NINE

MOLLY'S BREATH HITCHED in her throat as Dan angled his head to deepen the kiss. The crowd on the dance floor faded from her consciousness, making her feel as if there were only the two of them in the room. Nobody and nothing else mattered.

Dizzy with desire she pressed herself closer against him, wishing she could run her fingers over his muscles. Not that he didn't look absolutely amazing in a tux, because he did. But she still longed to touch him.

Abruptly he let her go, lifting his head and taking gulps of air. She smiled and rested her cheek against his chest. It was nice to know she wasn't the only one aroused beyond what was decent.

One song ran into the next until she had no idea how long they'd spent dancing. Or swaying, as, honestly, their feet didn't move much.

"Molly," Dan murmured, drawing her gaze. "As much as I don't want to stop, you should probably know the band is taking a break."

She stopped, and blushed when she realized they were the only ones still on the dance floor. "Oh."

"Are you hungry?" he asked, drawing her over toward where the buffet was set up.

She was, but not for food. "Not really. But I should try to find Kara." Guiltily, she remembered her friend.

"She's over there, standing next to David Jacobson." When she glanced over in the direction he indicated, she realized he was right. Kara caught her eye, raised her eyebrow and smiled, raising her champagne glass in a silent toast.

Molly knew the way she'd danced with Dan hadn't gone unnoticed, and she wanted to grimace at the thought of how Angel's grapevine would be rumbling with gossip by morning. But then again, she was single. And Dan was single. So what was the big deal?

"Do you want something else to drink?" he asked. She liked the way he kept an arm around her waist, leaning down to talk to her so that only she could hear him.

For the first time in too many months to

count she felt beautiful. Special. Sexy. She glanced up at the most good-looking guy in the entire room. "Dan, would you mind taking me home?"

"Of course not," he said, although she thought she saw a flash of disappointment in his eyes.

Obviously she hadn't made her meaning clear. She wanted him to take her home, but she didn't want him to leave.

She hoped he'd stay.

As they made their way toward the doorway, they were stopped along the way. "Dan, how are you?"

"Great, Marcus. Just great."

"And who's this pretty little thing?" Marcus asked, gazing at Molly with interest.

She couldn't help smiling when Dan's arm tightened around her waist. "This is Molly Shriver. Molly, Marcus is one of my colleagues."

"Nice to meet you," she said, dutifully shaking his hand.

"Excuse us, Marcus, but we need to leave. I'll check in with you next week, okay?" Dan drew her away, but before they cleared the ballroom they were stopped again, this time by Alex Rodriguez.

"You're not leaving already, are you?" Alex demanded.

"Afraid so. Alex, this is Molly Shriver. Molly, Alex Rodriguez is Head of Neurosurgery at Angel's."

"I'm familiar with Dr. Rodriguez, he refers lots of patients to me." She held out her hand, hiding a smile as Alex stared at her, obviously trying to place her name.

"Of course!" he finally exclaimed. "Molly Shriver, the physical therapist. It's great to meet you. You have an outstanding reputation."

"Thank you," she murmured, embarrassed at how much he was gushing over her. It was great to know she had recognition, even though no one apparently knew what she looked like. She was starting to feel a bit like a ghost.

"Did you hear the news?" Alex said in a low voice. "Layla Woods has been named the new Chief of General Pediatrics."

"Yeah, I heard," Dan said with a wry nod. "I was a little surprised but, then again, she has a decent reputation."

"I'm still not over the shock," Alex muttered, tossing back the rest of his champagne as if it were straight whiskey.

"You'll be fine," Dan said, clapping Alex on the shoulder. "Excuse us, we're just leaving."

They finally made it out of the ballroom without being stopped by any more of Dan's colleagues, and when they stepped outside, she shivered. "It's cold out here!"

Dan cuddled her close as he waited for his car to be brought out by the valet parking attendant. "Where's your coat, woman?" he asked, rubbing his hands up and down her arms in an effort to keep her warm.

"I wasn't going to buy a long coat for one evening," she said, half under her breath. Her waist-length jacket would have looked out of place with the emerald-green dress.

"Take mine," he said, shrugging out of his jacket and draping it around her shoulders.

Dan's sleek black BMW arrived less than five minutes later, and she slid into the passenger seat gratefully. Dan tipped the parking attendant and then climbed in beside her. He immediately cranked up the heat.

Now that they were alone in his car, nerves set in. What if he didn't want to come up to her apartment? What if he thought she lived in a dump? What if she'd misunderstood how he felt toward her? What if he wasn't as attracted to her as she was to him?

She'd initiated the kiss. Granted, he didn't pull away. In fact, he'd kissed her like he wasn't planning on stopping any time soon.

The memory was enough to make her heart race. She tried to take a deep breath to calm herself, but Dan must have noticed as he reached over to take her hand.

"Relax," he murmured. "Did I mention that Josh's nanny was spending the night at my place?"

For a moment she gaped at him. He tells her to relax and then he springs that on her? "She is, huh?"

"Yes, she is." A smile played around the corners of his mouth and that hint of humor was enough to make her relax.

Because she hadn't imagined his response to their kiss. "Sounds like it's your lucky night," she teased.

He tightened his fingers around hers. "You have no idea," he said in a husky tone.

"Oh, I think I do."

Thankfully, the drive to her apartment didn't take long. Finding parking, though, was another thing altogether. She was appalled at the fee he was forced to pay but, short of taking his car back to his place and taking the subway back, they didn't have a choice.

She unlocked the door and led the way inside. They didn't get very far when Dan caught her hand and pulled her close.

"Kiss me," he murmured.

She was happy to oblige. This time she slipped her hands beneath the jacket of his tux, causing him to groan low in his throat.

"Molly," he said between kisses. "Which way is your bedroom?"

"This way," she said breathlessly. Tearing herself away from him wasn't easy. As soon as they crossed the threshold of her bedroom, while she was thanking her lucky stars that she'd had the foresight to make her bed and clean up, his cell phone rang.

Dan froze, and looked down at her. "I'm sorry, Molly, but I need to make sure it's not about Josh," he said as he reached into his pocket for the phone.

"I understand." She made sure her disappointment wasn't reflected in her expression.

He glanced at the screen, sighed and pushed the button to answer the phone. "Gemma? Is everything all right?"

Molly could hear Gemma's reply. "Josh

is having a nightmare. He keeps calling for you."

"I'll be home in fifteen minutes." Dan snapped his phone shut and let out a heavy sigh. "Molly, I'm sorry, but Josh is calling for me and I really need to be there for him. I know the timing is terrible but for once he's not calling out for his mother."

"Don't be sorry. I totally understand." And she did understand—if Josh had been her son she'd leave in a heartbeat. "I'm okay, really."

Dan muttered what sounded like a curse as he ran his hand over his close-cropped hair. "Will you let me make it up to you? Say, with dinner tomorrow night?"

"That's not necessary—" she started to say, but he stopped her with a kiss.

"Yes, it is necessary," he said in a low, strained voice. "Very necessary. Please?"

How could she say no? "All right, call me tomorrow."

"Count on it." He kissed her again, and then turned to leave. She followed him to the door, making sure she locked it after he left.

She leaned against the door, wondering if she'd truly lost her mind. She couldn't sleep with Dan. He was a big-shot open-heart surgeon at Angel's!

Not to mention the father of her patient. But that argument didn't hold much weight as she wouldn't be Josh's therapist forever.

Still, what did she have to offer someone like Dan? Nothing that he couldn't get with any other woman and, heaven knew, New York was full of single women, any of whom would be thrilled to be with someone like Dan.

She couldn't bear it if he abandoned her the same way James had.

If she was smart, she'd find an excuse to avoid seeing him again.

If she was smart, she'd stop the madness before she got hurt.

Dan was grateful Josh's nightmare had pretty much faded by the time he'd gotten home from Molly's, but he stayed up for a while longer, making sure his son was resting quietly before he crawled into his own bed.

Falling asleep wasn't easy, though, as he still ached for Molly. He almost considered heading back over there, but knew that wasn't fair. She'd be asleep by now, and even if she wasn't, Josh might wake up again. No, he couldn't take the risk. Besides, she'd already agreed to go to dinner with him on Saturday night. Tonight, as it was already past midnight.

He wasted a good hour staring up at his ceiling, thinking about where to take her. He wanted her to feel comfortable, yet he also wanted the evening to be special. He thought of the perfect place and finally fell asleep.

Thankfully, Gemma let him sleep in, taking care of Josh until he crawled out of bed. After he finished in the bathroom, Josh came to greet him. "Hi, Daddy."

"Hi, Josh." He was thrilled to realize his relationship with his son had gotten so much better and was deeply touched that Josh had called out for him in the night and not his mother. He swept the boy into his arms for a hug.

"Gemma's in the kitchen," Josh said importantly.

"Have you already eaten breakfast?" he asked.

Josh nodded. "Yep."

"I hope you left me some, 'cos I'm hungry," he confided, heading toward the kitchen. As he approached, he heard Gemma on the phone with her daughter. "Sure, honey, I'll be happy to babysit tonight."

No! Wait! He needed Gemma tonight! He

rushed forward but too late. When she hung up the phone, he knew he was out of luck.

"Good morning, Dr. Morris. Now that you're up, I'm going to leave. I have a lot of things to do today."

It took everything he had to smile. "No problem. I take it you're babysitting tonight for your granddaughter?"

"Yes, I love spending time with Emily. My daughter and her husband want to go out for dinner," she admitted, sealing his fate.

Dammit, he wanted to go out for dinner, too!

"Well, have fun, then." He watched her leave and then scrubbed his hand over his bristly jaw. He didn't want to cancel his plans with Molly, but what choice did he have? Unless he could find another babysitter?

He didn't want to leave Josh with a stranger, so he went back to his list of former nannies and found the number for Betsy, the one Josh liked best.

Unfortunately, Betsy was busy. So he went down the list. After calling several former nannies without success, he was about to give up when Josh's tutor called to follow up on Josh's progress.

"Mitch, I know you're a tutor and not a

babysitter, but would you be willing to stay here tonight with Josh?"

"I have a biochemistry exam on Monday, so my only plans were to study, so why not? I can always study after Josh falls asleep."

Dan closed his eyes and thanked his lucky stars that Mitch had a biochem exam rather than a date that night. "Thanks, I'll pay you your tutoring fee for the entire night."

"Heck, Dr. Morris, that's not necessary. The standard babysitting fee is fine."

"I insist." Dan could barely contain his excitement. Not only was he going to see Molly again tonight but Josh would be in good hands with Mitch.

A win-win situation all the way around.

He ate a quick breakfast and then called to make reservations at Valencia's, a very small yet expensive restaurant that he'd stumbled upon by accident several years ago. Once he'd finalized his arrangements, he dialed Molly's number, feeling more nervous than he had in a long time. She didn't answer, so he left a message.

"Hi, Molly, I've made reservations tonight for eight o'clock. I'll pick you up at seven-thirty if that's okay. Please give me a call back to confirm."

Having finished up what he needed to do, he went over to help himself to more coffee. He glanced up as Josh rolled his wheelchair into the room.

"Can we play Molly's games, Daddy? Can we?"

He nodded, squelching a flash of guilt at knowing he'd leave Josh with Mitch tonight. So he decided to make sure Josh had a lot of fun today. "Sure thing. And afterward we can go to another movie if you'd like."

"Really?" Josh's face lit up like a neon sign. "Awesome."

He sipped his coffee and waited, figuring Josh was going to ask again about inviting Molly along, but when Josh didn't, he decided to count that as another win.

It was humbling to realize his son didn't mind spending time with him alone now.

And he vowed to make sure that even once he went back to work, he'd still set aside plenty of family time with Josh. Maybe he hadn't known much about love and family when he and Suzy had first got married, but he was determined to rectify that mistake.

Josh would always know what it was like to be loved. And wanted. Not like an inconvenience, the way his mother had treated him.

His own mother had blamed him for ruining her life after his father, an officer in the army, had died in Vietnam. Granted, his mother had gotten pregnant on purpose so that her officer would marry her, but being pregnant and widowed at the age of nineteen had been far more than she'd bargained for.

And throughout the years she'd made sure Dan had known that her misery was all his fault. Thankfully, he'd been able to lose himself in books and later in his studies, earning him the title of valedictorian of his high school graduating class.

He'd been lucky, he realized now, that he'd earned a full ride at New York's top university. He'd worked hard to get where he was today, but somehow, with all he'd accomplished, he still felt empty. As if there was something inside him that made him unlovable.

Sure, Josh loved him. But Suzy hadn't. And his mother certainly hadn't.

Playing with Josh eased his thoughts about his upbringing, and as they played Molly's kick-the-ball game, he was amazed that Josh was able to move his legs from side to side with far more strength than he had previously.

For the first time in a long while he began to believe that Josh really might walk again.

His phone rang, and he jumped up off the floor, nearly tripping over his own two feet in his haste to answer it. When he saw the caller was Molly, he ducked into the kitchen for some privacy.

"Hi, Molly, how are you?"

"I'm good, thanks. How's Josh?"

"He's fine. Slept well after his nightmare and seems to be back to normal today."

"That's good. I'm sure that it was hard on you not being there for him."

"Yes. But it was hard leaving you, too."

There was an awkward pause and his gut clenched with fear. Was she going to try and cancel on him?

When she didn't answer, he spoke in a rush. "Josh's tutor Mitch has agreed to stay here tonight, so I hope the dinner plans I made are okay with you."

"Oh, that's wonderful. I'm glad Josh will be spending time with Mitch. Dinner sounds good and I'll be ready by seven-thirty."

His shoulders sagged with relief. She hadn't cancelled their plans. "Great! I'm really looking forward to seeing you again."

"Me, too," she admitted in a voice so soft

he had to strain to hear her. "I have to go, but I'll see you later, okay?"

"Sure thing." He hung up the phone, knowing there was a goofy smile plastered on his face but unable to find the energy to care.

He believed Molly cared about him, and not because he was a surgeon. Like him, she'd been hurt in the past, and he found he was desperate to see her again. To share a nice, romantic dinner together. Only this time, with a little luck, they wouldn't be interrupted by any sort of crisis.

He could hardly wait.

Molly had spent the morning lecturing herself on getting involved with Dan more than she already was, and had fully intended to back out of their tentative dinner plans. But once she had been on the phone with him, she hadn't been able to do it. For one thing, he'd already arranged for a babysitter, and she was glad that Josh would have fun with Mitch.

But the real reason she didn't back out was because once she heard his deep voice resonating in her ear she realized how much she wanted to see him again. She'd been thinking about Dan when she'd fallen asleep, and he'd been the first thing on her mind when she'd woken up.

Doomed, she thought with a wry shake of her head. She was doomed and too far gone to turn back now.

Sally had called to apologize for embarrassing her at the fund-raiser. Of course Molly accepted her apology and they'd ended the call on better terms. But deep down she knew she and Sally would never be as close as blood sisters.

Or even sisters of the heart.

Dan would say that was Sally's loss and she wanted to believe he was right. But she was the one who'd always wanted a family. Sally had no idea how lucky she was to have parents who doted on her and a fiancé who loved and adored her.

Enough with the pity party! She spent the rest of the morning cleaning her tiny apartment, which obviously didn't take long, and then took the subway to do some window shopping.

She couldn't really afford to buy another dress for her dinner tonight with Dan, but that didn't stop her from looking. She found lots of cute dresses, but in the end she decided to wear her old standby black skirt with a nice teal-colored sweater.

She was ready to leave well before seven, and tried to read, but ended up nervously pacing the tiny length of her apartment instead.

When her buzzer rang at exactly seven-thirty, she grabbed her coat and purse before crossing over to the intercom. "I'll be right down."

She took the elevator and caught her breath when she saw that Dan was dressed in a pair of charcoal-grey slacks and a black crew-neck sweater. Although she liked the way he filled out a tux, she was finding that she liked the way he looked no matter what he wore. "Hi," she greeted him shyly.

"Hi, Molly." He gave her a hug, surrounding her with his musky scent mingled with a hint of aftershave. "You look fantastic."

"Thank you." She didn't bother telling him how he'd now seen the full extent of her dressy wardrobe.

He opened the car door for her, and after sliding in she had to smile when she noticed that once again he'd cranked up the heat for her. Taking pity on him, she turned the knob down a few notches.

"I want you to know that Josh's leg muscles

are getting stronger," he said, as he swung into the traffic. "We played kick the ball and he did amazingly well."

"That's great news," she said with a smile. "See, I told you the games were worth it," she teased.

"Yes, you did." She was surprised when Dan reached out to take her hand. "And you were right, I should have trusted in your judgment all along. I don't know how I'll ever be able to repay you."

"No payment necessary," she murmured. "There's nothing more rewarding than watching a patient's progress toward his or her goals. It's one of the reasons I love my job."

"And you're damn good at it, too," he said, still holding her hand.

She smiled. "I told you so," she teased as he put his hand back on the steering wheel. But she couldn't help feeling a twinge of regret at knowing that her time with Josh and Dan would eventually come to an end.

All too soon they wouldn't need her anymore.

"Hey, what's wrong?" he asked, as if sensing her disquiet.

"Nothing." She pushed the melancholy

away. "In fact, my sister called me today and apologized for her behavior at the Ritz."

Dan's lips thinned. "She should apologize," he muttered ungraciously. "She had no right to hurt you like that."

She was touched by his concern on her behalf. "She doesn't mean to hurt me, it's really my problem. I've never felt as if I was part of the family."

He glanced at her. "I'm sure they adopted you for a reason, Molly."

"Yes, but shortly after they brought me home they found out they were pregnant with Sally, and from then on things changed." She lifted a shoulder in a careless shrug. "She became the center of their world, and I was more of an afterthought. Still, I know I should be grateful for what I have. I could have easily been sent from one foster home to another."

He was quiet for a long moment. "I'm sorry that you had that experience, Molly. But living with a blood relative, a mother who gave birth to you, doesn't automatically bring unconditional love," he said. "Unfortunately, some people just aren't capable of feeling that deeply about anyone else."

His words stopped her cold, and she had the distinct impression he was talking from personal experience. About his own mother? Or just his ex who had married him and given birth to Josh yet hadn't loved either one of them enough to stay?

"I feel sorry for those people, Dan. They'll never know what they've missed." She reached over and took his hand, vowing to prove to him that his ex had been stupid and wrong.

He and Josh were both special and very much deserved to be loved and cared for.

CHAPTER TEN

Dan was touched when Molly reached for his hand, and he mentally cursed himself for allowing talk of their respective pasts to dampen the mood. He wanted tonight to be special. No sadness or regret allowed.

He gave her fingers a gentle squeeze. "Hey, will you please do me a favor?" She glanced at him in surprise, nodding automatically. "Smile, Molly. I want tonight to be about us, two people having a nice time together. I want you to have fun tonight."

She smiled and just like that the shadow that hovered over his soul was gone. "All right. So tell me, where is this place you're taking me?"

"Valencia's." He grinned. "It's one of the best-kept secrets. They have great seafood and they're located in the West Village."

"Sounds perfect."

"Have you ever eaten there before?" He didn't want to assume she hadn't. For all he knew, that guy she'd been seeing had taken her there. The thought made him scowl.

"No, although I've heard wonderful things about it."

Selfishly, he was glad she hadn't been there before. He parked his car at a very expensive structure and they walked the rest of the way.

"Oh, my gosh, this is a cobblestone street!" Molly said with a gasp of surprise.

"Yeah, this is a colonial building that was once used as a carriage house." He put his hand in the small of her back as she walked into the restaurant.

"Wow, fancy," she whispered, as they waited to be greeted by the maître d'.

"We have an eight-o'clock reservation," he said. "Dan Morris."

"Of course, Dr. Morris. Right this way, sir. You requested a table by the fireplace, correct?"

"Yes. Thank you." He smiled when Molly took the seat closest to the fire. "Would you like wine?" he asked. "Or maybe you'd prefer champagne?"

Molly blushed, or maybe it was the heat from the fire. "Wine would be great. I think

I should stay away from champagne for a while."

"Do you have a wine preference?" he asked, studying the wine list.

"Anything you choose is fine with me."

He ordered a French red wine and watched Molly peruse the menu. Her eyes were as wide as saucers as she glanced over the options.

"The prices are outrageous," she whispered in horror.

"Molly, relax. Splurge a little." He hadn't brought her here to intimidate her—he wanted her to enjoy herself. "What would you have if money was no object?"

She worried her lower lip between her teeth, making him want to kiss her. "I have a secret love of lobster," she confessed. "And I also love a good steak."

"Then have both," he urged. "I promise you'll love it."

They placed their order and he noticed Molly relax as she sipped her wine. "This is very nice, Dan. Thanks for bringing me."

"You're more than welcome. Besides, you deserve special treatment. Do you have any idea what a great reputation you have at Angel's?"

She arched a brow. "Do you have any idea what a great reputation *you* have at Angel's?" she countered. "Your patients love you."

"So do yours." He reached across to take her hand in his. "Your bright, sunny attitude is amazing. I don't think I've ever met anyone who enjoyed their work as much as you do."

She blushed and took a sip of her wine. "I'm sure you enjoy your work," she countered. "Saving small children's lives by doing open-heart surgery is far more important than what I do each day."

He cocked his head to the side, wishing he could find a way to convince her how special she was. "Your work is just as important. We both give hope to our small patients and their parents."

"Giving hope," she murmured with a smile. "I like that comparison, even if you're exaggerating my expertise."

"Molly, believe me when I say that no woman has ever talked to me the way you did after Josh's first therapy session," he said with a wry grin. "Your passion for your work is unsurpassed by anyone I've ever met."

"I let my temper get away from me," she admitted with a deep blush, making him want nothing more but to take her into his arms.

But the waiter arrived with their first course and he had to settle for watching Molly enjoy her salad.

"What made you decide to become a pediatric heart surgeon?" she asked, when she'd finished.

Unwilling to ruin the mood, he gave her the light version. "I always wanted to be a doctor, and once I started my surgical residency I knew cardiothoracic surgery was my area of expertise. Yet once I finished my pediatric rotation I knew that working with kids was equally important. Luckily, I landed a job at Angel's that allows me to do the most with my little bit of talent."

"Little bit of talent?" she echoed dryly. "I say you're underestimating your ability."

"Giving kids the opportunity to have a normal life is important to me." He stared at his empty salad plate for a moment. "Yet I almost screwed up with Josh, big time."

"Josh loves you," she protested quickly.

He forced a smile. "Yeah, we're getting back on track. And I'm thrilled he's getting stronger every day. Today we went to another movie and for the first time in a long time he didn't ask for you to come with us." When he realized how that might have sounded, he tried to backpedal. "I mean, he loves having you around, but—"

She interrupted him with a laugh. "Don't worry, I understand. It's okay, he should want to spend time with you. You're his father."

As he gazed at Molly across the table, her red-and-gold hair glowing from the light of the fire, he realized that Molly would be an excellent mother. Far better than Suzy. Far better than his own.

And he was one lucky son of a gun to be here with her. Especially when she had no idea how unique and special she was.

He was sure his food tasted wonderful, but he didn't really pay much attention, having more fun watching Molly as she enjoyed every aspect of their meal.

He forced her to split the chocolate mousse for dessert and longed to lean forward to taste the chocolate from her lips instead of just from the spoon.

After they finished dinner, he followed her back outside to his car. "Thanks for the lovely dinner, Dan," she said as they approached his car.

He hoped, prayed the night wasn't over yet, but he didn't say anything as he closed her passenger door behind her and then walked around to slide into the driver's seat.

The ride back across town to her apartment didn't take long. When he was within a block or two of the parking garage he glanced over at her, feeling a little bit panicked at the thought of letting her go. "Molly, I don't want the evening to end."

She went still, before she glanced up at him. "Is that your way of asking if you can come up?"

His gut clenched. "Yes, Molly. I want to come up with you, spend the night making love with you. But only if that's what you want, too."

When she didn't answer right away, he figured he'd pushed too hard. But then she nodded. "I'd like that," she murmured in a low voice.

He let out his breath in a soundless sigh. Last night they'd been carried away by the slow dancing and champagne. Tonight it was a deliberate decision, on his part and on hers. One that he didn't want her to regret.

"I'm so glad," he said. "I was afraid you were going to make me beg."

"Never," she murmured with a laugh, and the last of his tension eased away.

He'd never looked forward to being with anyone the way he wanted to be with Molly.

Molly couldn't believe Dan had spoken so bluntly about how he wanted to spend the rest of their night. As they rode the elevator up to her apartment, she was tempted to pinch herself to make sure she wasn't dreaming. He'd been so wonderful, so attentive at dinner. For the first time in so long she felt beautiful, special.

And she wanted to hold on to that feeling for at least a little while longer.

She couldn't believe this was a mistake. Not when it felt so right. They were going to make love. She knew it. He knew it. For some reason, inviting him up last night had been easier but, oddly enough, she found tonight to be more romantic.

At least now she knew that he truly wanted her. Almost as much as she wanted him.

Still, she was nervous about taking this step, knowing that once they made love there was no going back. As they stepped into her apartment, she mentally kicked herself for not going out to buy some wine today, rather than window shopping.

"I only have soft drinks to offer you," she

said apologetically, when he'd closed the apartment door. She turned to go into the minuscule kitchen to get something for them to drink out of the fridge.

"Molly…" The way he said her name made her heart melt, and when he stopped her and pulled her close she didn't resist. "I didn't come here for something to drink. I came here for you."

Before she could say anything more, he lowered his head and kissed her. Instantly, she forgot everything except how much she loved his mouth taking possession of hers.

Somehow he slid her coat off without her knowing, gathering her close as he deepened the kiss. She clung to his broad shoulders, enjoying the combination of sweetness and strength.

When he lifted his head and led her down the hall toward her bedroom, she gasped for breath and tried to gather her scattered thoughts.

"Are you sure Josh is all right?" she asked, when they entered her bedroom. Was she crazy to be here with him like this? "Maybe you should check on him."

Dan yanked her close and kissed her again. "Are you stalling?" he asked a minute or so later. "Nothing short of a tornado is going to stop me from making love to you tonight."

She laughed, but then her mouth went dry when he gently pulled her sweater up and over her head. In mere seconds he'd loosened the waistband of her skirt until the garment fell and pooled at her feet. Her bra and panties quickly followed.

For a moment she wanted to cover herself, but then his eyes darkened as he gazed at her. "You're so incredibly beautiful, Molly," he said in a voice husky with need.

She couldn't speak, but tugged at his clothes until he was as naked as she was. And then he kissed her, and kept kissing her, even as he picked her up and carried her over to the bed.

Warmth radiated from his skin and she trailed her hands up and over his biceps, enjoying the sensation of springy hair as she reached his chest, softening the strong muscles. She loved being able to touch him. All over.

Everywhere.

When she trailed her hands down to his magnificent butt, he growled low in his throat and left a trail of kisses as he made his way down to her breast.

She gasped and arched her back when he licked and suckled her nipple. Moving restlessly beneath him, she tried to pull him closer.

"Plenty of time," he murmured between kissing the tip of one breast and then the other. "I want to taste every inch."

Dear heaven, she wanted that, too.

"Molly." He lifted his head and stared at her. "You're sure about this, right? You haven't changed your mind?"

And just like that her nervousness faded away. She reached up to rest her palm against the side of his face, the same caress he'd given her after falling out of his wheelchair. "Yes, I'm sure. I haven't changed my mind."

"Thank God," he muttered, and lowered his head once again to her breast.

And then all ability to think vanished as he proceeded to make good on his promise to kiss her all over.

Molly closed her eyes and hugged Dan close as their ragged breathing gradually slowed. The intensity of his lovemaking was unlike anything she'd experienced in her entire life.

After a few minutes Dan groaned and rolled over onto his side, taking her with him, apparently unwilling to let her go. She tucked her head into the hollow of his shoulder, and inhaled deeply, filling her nose with his scent.

She must have dozed even though she hadn't intended to. But she woke up when she felt Dan ease away from her and roll off the bed.

"Where are you going?" she asked, before she could bite her tongue.

"I'm sorry, I didn't mean to wake you."

She clutched the sheet to her chest and squinted toward the blue illuminated numbers on her alarm clock. "It's barely five o'clock in the morning."

"I know, but I need to get home before Josh wakes up." He sounded apologetic but drew on his clothes. "I was trying to decide if I should wake you up or just let you sleep."

He'd obviously chosen the latter, although he couldn't know she was an extremely light sleeper. She tried not to feel bad that he was leaving. Logically, she knew he needed to get home to his son. For some foolish reason she'd envisioned them sharing a quiet breakfast together.

"Go back to sleep, Molly," he murmured, leaning over to kiss her. "I'll call you later on today, all right?"

"Sure." She forced herself to get up and grab her robe, so that she could lock the apartment door behind him. She clutched the lapel tight and tried to smile. "Good night, Dan."

"Good night, Molly." He kissed her again before he left. And she locked the door behind him and went back to bed.

But she didn't sleep. Being all alone in the aftermath of the intense pleasure they'd shared brought all her earlier doubts back. Had he been anxious to leave? Had he planned all along to leave before she'd woken up? Was he regretting staying with her even as long as he had? Had he realized she was nothing more than a plain Jane with nothing special to offer?

Had she just made the biggest mistake of her life?

It was entirely possible, because right now she felt worse than the day James had told her that he loved someone else.

Molly got up and made herself a bowl of cereal and a pot of coffee. She read through the Sunday paper, determined to keep up with the news. After she'd completed a few loads of laundry, she decided to go over to see Dan and Josh. She didn't call ahead, simply deciding to take the subway.

She got off at the stop that was near Angel's and paused for a moment to gaze up at the impressive hospital overlooking Central Park. The history of the hospital's origin was humbling. Back in the dark days after the Depression, after his little boy had died of polio, Federico Mendez had established New York's first children's hospital, known for giving charity care to those children in need. In the years since then Angel's had become well known all across the country. Rich or poor, every child in New York was welcome to be cared for at Angel's. Even on Sunday it was busy, and she watched a medical helicopter land on the roof, no doubt bringing another small patient to Angel's house of hope.

She started walking toward Dan's condo, but stopped abruptly when she caught sight of two people in wheelchairs heading down the sidewalk on the other side of the street. She recognized Dan and Josh, arms pumping hard as they propelled their wheelchairs down toward the park.

She stepped back so they wouldn't see her, and watched as Josh laughed when he pulled ahead of his father. They were obviously enjoying some father-and-son time, which was good.

After watching Dan and Josh head into the park, she turned and retraced her steps to the subway. She shouldn't feel disappointed that they hadn't included her. Wasn't this what she'd wanted all along? For Josh and Dan to become close?

When she'd been with James, he'd always included her in all family outings. She could look back now and realize he'd used her more or less as a surrogate mother for his sons. They really hadn't had very much alone time as a couple. Which hadn't exactly helped their personal relationship. Was it any wonder they'd grown apart? Was it any wonder he'd fallen in love with someone else?

She should be glad that Dan wasn't doing the same thing. Obviously, he'd made love to her last night because he'd wanted to. He'd arranged for a babysitter so he could take her to a lovely dinner. So why did she still feel left out?

Determined to stop wallowing in self-pity, she headed over to see her parents. They always had a standing Sunday brunch invitation and today she'd surprise everyone by stopping by.

Twenty-five minutes later she arrived at her parents' place and wasn't entirely surprised to find Sally and Mike there, as well.

"Molly, it's so good to see you," her mother said, giving her a big hug. She clung to her mother for a long minute, before letting go to hug her father.

"It's good to see you, too," she said, hoping they didn't notice the dampness around her eyes. "Hi, Sally, Mike. How are your wedding plans coming along?"

"Wonderful!" Sally said, as they gathered in the kitchen. "We have our church and the hall picked out."

"Really? And when's the big day?" Molly helped herself to a glass of orange juice.

"August twenty-first. We were lucky that the hall had a cancelation."

"Wow, that's only a few months away," she murmured. Obviously the wedding plans had been going on for quite a while.

"Food's ready," her mother called.

Even though the conversation centered around Sally and Mike's upcoming wedding, Molly was glad to be here, surrounded by her family. For a brief time she didn't feel so much like an outsider.

Although she couldn't help thinking about

Dan and Josh. Wondering how they were spending their day. Had they gone to another movie after their trip to the park? Or had they gone back to Fun and Games?

It was ridiculous to keep thinking about them when she'd see them both the following morning.

She stayed at her parents' house as long as she could, before heading back home.

There was no message from Dan waiting for her, and she wondered if he'd regretted spending the night with her.

Had he said those nice things to her at dinner just to get her into bed? Had she been hopelessly naive to believe him? Her stomach clenched as she couldn't help thinking the worst, especially as it was clear that he hadn't followed through with his promise to call.

It was her fault for getting emotionally involved with Dan in the first place. And it would be up to her to get over him, the same way she'd managed to get over James.

One painful day at a time.

CHAPTER ELEVEN

DAN CALLED MOLLY a half-dozen times, but when she didn't answer he hung up before her machine kicked in. He didn't want to leave a message. After the way he'd been forced to leave earlier that morning, she deserved better than to hear him say *"I'm thinking of you"* on a machine.

Leaving her warm bed had been one of the hardest things he'd ever done. If not for Josh being home with Mitch, he would have stayed longer. The rest of the weekend, if she'd have let him.

He ran his hands over his hair and told himself Molly wouldn't hold being a single father against him. After all, she loved kids. She understood that he'd needed to get home for Josh.

So why did he feel as if he'd let her down?

After he'd returned home, he'd caught another couple of hours of sleep before the rest of the household had gotten up. Once they'd eaten breakfast, Mitch had left to return home and he'd decided to celebrate the mild weather by taking Josh down to Central Park. They'd both used their wheelchairs, much to Josh's amusement.

As much as he tried to spend quality father-and-son time with Josh, he'd often become distracted by thoughts of Molly. He couldn't remember the last time a woman had dominated his thoughts.

Suzy didn't count as she'd once dominated his thoughts in a bad way. Molly's fresh laughter was the complete antithesis of Suzy's bitterness.

Yet he was forced to admit that maybe some of his ex's bitterness had been justified. He had worked a lot of hours. He could have spent more time with her. At the time he'd thought maybe he simply wasn't capable of love.

But being with Molly and Josh proved that theory to be false. He loved Josh. And he cared deeply for Molly. He knew she cared, at least a little, about him, too.

Maybe he wasn't so unlovable after all.

Once they'd returned home from Central

Park, he spent some time working on Josh's surprise birthday party, and he called Molly again.

This time she answered. "Hello?"

"Finally we get to talk," he said. "I've been getting your machine most of the day."

"Really? Why didn't you leave a message?"

"Because I wanted to talk to you." And now that he was talking to her, his nerves settled down. He took the phone into the other room, out of Josh's hearing. "How are you? What have you been up to?"

"Had brunch with my parents, ran a few errands. The usual."

Was it his imagination or did she seem to be a tiny bit standoffish? Was she upset with him? "I wish I could have stayed with you this morning," he murmured. "I wish you were here right now."

There was a moment of silence before she spoke again. "I've been thinking of you, too."

The admission made him feel better. "I'd like to see you again. Soon."

"You and Josh are coming to therapy in the morning, aren't you?" she asked in a teasing tone.

"Yes. But what I meant is that I want to

see you alone. Maybe we can do dinner one night this week?"

Another small silence and he wished she were here in front of him so he could read her facial expressions. He didn't like having to second-guess her thoughts. "I don't know if that will work. I generally try not to stay up too late on work nights."

Was she really worried about getting up for work in the morning? Or was she trying to put distance between them? "How about Friday night, then? Josh's party is on Saturday and it would be easier if you just stayed here overnight. You can sleep in the spare bedroom, if you're worried about Josh being here."

"Hmm, let me think about that," she said evasively. "Speaking of Josh's birthday, how is the party planning coming along?"

"Great." He injected enthusiasm into his voice when really just the thought of being in charge of all those kids was as daunting as hell. "Most of the kids in his class have responded that they're coming, which makes me feel better."

"Oh, Dan, that's great news." Molly's excitement was contagious. "Josh is going to have a wonderful time, you'll see."

"And he'll owe it all to you for coming up with the idea." He gripped the phone tighter and wished once again she was there with him. Especially when she laughed softly.

"No, you need to take the credit for having this party, not me. After all, you're doing all the work." There was a brief silence, and then she added, "I have to get going. See you tomorrow, Dan."

"All right. See you tomorrow, Molly." He disconnected the call, wondering how he was going to manage to wait until Friday night to be alone with her again.

Molly did her best to keep things on a professional level when she saw Josh and Dan the following morning. She was already too close to falling for him, and didn't want to make the same mistakes she'd made in the past. But it wasn't easy when Dan stood close, his arm lightly brushing hers.

She eased away, concentrating on Josh. "Wow, you're doing very well, Josh. Look at how high you can kick your feet!"

Josh beamed. "We've been practicing, right, Dad?"

"Right," Dan agreed.

She was glad, very glad that the two of

them were so comfortable around each other now. A far cry from their first day of therapy, that's for sure. She went through her list of warm-up games, and then decided it was time to move onto the next step.

"Okay, now we're going to try to stand again," she said, gesturing for Josh to follow her in his wheelchair over to the small platform nestled between parallel bars. "Are you ready, Freddie?"

Josh giggled, as she'd hoped he would. "I'm not Freddie," he said, as he set the brakes on his wheelchair.

"Are you sure? Because you look like a Freddie." She was proud at how bravely he faced the challenge of standing. His leg muscles were getting stronger, but they still had a way to go before he would be walking again.

Although there wasn't any doubt in her mind that he would accomplish that task.

"Wait for me," she said quickly, when Josh pushed up on the padded armrests of his wheelchair. His upper-arm strength had grown by leaps and bounds since Dan had agreed to let him use a wheelchair. "Steady now," she warned, as he stood up on his own two feet.

Josh didn't say anything, his face scrunched

up with fierce concentration. She put her elbow under his armpit and took some of his weight.

"I can do it myself," he said testily.

"Okay." She eased back, allowing him to support his own weight but staying close by in case he lost his balance.

"Look, Dad," Josh said excitedly when he managed to grip the parallel bars and balance between them. "I can stand!"

"You sure can, Josh," Dan said in a husky voice. Molly didn't dare take her eyes off Josh to look over at him, but she knew he had to be thrilled with Josh's progress.

"How are your legs feeling?" she asked. His muscles were quivering beneath the strain, but he seemed determined to stay upright.

"Fine," he claimed, although the quivering got worse.

She waited a full minute before stepping forward. "Okay, Josh, let's have you sit back down, slow and easy."

He didn't argue this time, and soon he was seated once again in his wheelchair.

Dan came over and crouched beside Josh. "I'm so proud of you, Josh. Your hard work is really paying off. The way your leg muscles are getting stronger is nothing short of amazing."

"Thanks, Dad," Josh said, throwing his arms around his father's neck and squeezing tightly.

Molly had to blink back tears, watching the way father and son clung to each other. And then Josh pulled back and glanced up at Molly. "Is it time for the massage yet?" he asked.

She had to laugh. "I suspect that's your favorite part of the day," she teased, as she headed over to the table set up near the ultrasound machine. "Either that or you just want to get through the rest of your therapy so that you can pick out a lollipop."

"I'm betting it's both," Dan said with a broad smile.

As she started her massage Dan's cell phone rang. He glanced at the screen, frowned and then glanced at her. "My colleague Marcus," he said, before he left the room to take the call.

She wondered why Marcus was calling. Did he have a question about patient care? Did they often talk about their respective patients?

Dan was still on the phone when she finished with Josh's massage and then moved on to the ultrasound treatments. She'd finished one leg and had started on the other when he finally returned, his expression grim.

"Problems?" she asked.

"Sort of. There's apparently a particularly challenging patient who needs surgery," he admitted.

She sensed he didn't want to talk in front of Josh, so she refrained from asking more as she finished up the ultrasound treatments. "All finished," she said cheerfully, as she put the machine away and began scraping the gel from Josh's legs. "Are you ready for a lolli-pop?"

Josh nodded and then contemplated the fla-vors left in the candy jar. "Grape," he said, pulling out the last one. He wasted no time in tearing off the purple wrapper and popping the candy in his mouth.

"Molly, do you have a minute?" Dan asked in a low voice.

"Sure." She turned to Josh. "I'll be right back, okay?"

Josh nodded, sucking on his lollipop with such force that his cheeks were sunk in, mak-ing him look like a fish.

"What's wrong?" she asked, the moment they were alone.

"I need to return to work," Dan said. "I was planning to be off this week, but unfortunately this patient can't wait."

She hid her dismay, knowing better than to ask for specifics. "Who will bring Josh to therapy?"

"Gemma, his nanny, or maybe Mitch." Dan blew out a breath and shook his head. "You need to understand that I wouldn't make a decision like this lightly. This patient needs my expertise, or I wouldn't cut my leave of absence short."

Deep down, she wanted to ask why Marcus couldn't do the surgery, but she managed to hold her tongue. After all, what Dan chose to do wasn't really her business.

One night together didn't mean much in the big scheme of things.

"Just make sure you keep spending time with Josh," she said lightly. "Because he needs a father as much as your patients need a top-notch surgeon."

"I know. Watching him stand was amazing. After the accident…" He paused then cleared his throat before continuing, "I don't know if

I'd be able to forgive myself for that brief moment of inattentiveness just before the crash."

"Oh, Dan, it's not your fault," she soothed, trying to make him understand. "Your car was T-boned because the other driver ran a red light." She remembered reading about the crash in the newspaper. Scary stuff.

"Thanks for saying that," he murmured. He stared at her for a long moment, as if he wanted to say something more, but then turned away. She followed him back to where Josh was already waiting for them in his wheelchair.

"Goodbye, Josh, I'll see you tomorrow."

"Bye, Molly." Josh waved cheerfully, before following his father out of the door. She watched them leave, wondering what Josh's reaction would be once he discovered his father was planning to return to work.

Her heart ached for him. And for herself.

Because she couldn't help being afraid that once Dan was fully entrenched back in his old life, he'd revert back to his old ways. Being stern and serious, rather than taking the time to enjoy life. Yet he'd promised to maintain his relationship with his son, so she tried to take comfort in that thought.

Of course Josh would always come first.

Which was the way it should be. And if he didn't have time for her, then obviously a relationship between them wasn't meant to be.

Dan went to the hospital early on Tuesday morning, and it seemed strange to walk through the lobby of Angel's after being gone for so long. His long white coat flapped against his thighs as he quickened his pace to reach the elevator.

He hurried up to the labor and delivery unit, where a pregnant woman was about to give birth to a baby with tetralogy of Fallot, a birth defect in which the infant's heart was essentially turned backward in its tiny chest. Normally this type of condition required surgery at some point during the baby's first year of life, but in this instance the unborn baby had been diagnosed with an additional complication, hydroplastic pulmonary arteries, which required bypass surgery to assist in oxygenating the infant's lungs. In years past these babies died, but now they could be operated on as soon as the infant was born and these children were now living well into their thirties and beyond.

The biggest catch was that the complex bypass procedure had to be started as soon as the baby was born or the child would die. And it was easily a ten- to twelve-hour procedure.

When he arrived in the labor and delivery suite, there was already a group of physicians and nurses filling the room. One of the nurses noticed him. "The cardiothoracic surgeon is here," she announced.

"Good. Nice to see you again, Dan. If everyone is ready, let's get this show on the road," Rebecca Kramer said briskly, pushing forward the gurney with the pregnant mother.

Rebecca Kramer was one of the neonatology experts on staff at Angel's and they'd worked together before, but there wasn't time for small talk as Dan could tell by the fetal monitor tracing that the baby was in trouble. They'd planned this C-section early, and it was obviously a good thing as it seemed the baby would have been born today, regardless. He made several phone calls of his own, making sure the O.R. right next to the one that Rebecca would use was equipped with what he'd need for long, grueling open-heart surgery.

"I want to see my baby," the pregnant woman sobbed, as they wheeled her into the O.R. suite. "I want to see her, to hold her in my arms before she has surgery."

Dan was used to this request, and had to

steel his heart against her pleading gaze. He glanced at her name on her hospital bracelet. "I'm sorry, Mrs. Thompson, but your baby girl won't live if we wait," he said gently. "Have you chosen a name for her yet?"

"Erica," she said with a sob. "Erica Marie. After my husband, Eric. He's stationed in Iraq. Are you sure we can't wait for him? He's on his way home, he promised to be here soon."

"I'm sorry, but we can't wait. The minute Erica is born we're going to start surgery. The quicker we get started, the better her outcome will be. I've had a lot of success, so you and your husband just need to be patient, okay?"

She nodded, but tears continued to stream down her cheeks. "Okay."

He scrubbed while they prepped the pregnant mother's belly. Jennifer Thompson wanted to be awake during the C-section so the anesthesiologist topped up her epidural. There was a sense of urgency in both O.R. suites because there wasn't a moment to waste. Lives were on the line and as always the staff of Angel's took the care of their young patients very seriously.

He was gowned, gloved and masked when he heard the shout. "We have the baby out."

"We're ready," he called back. And seconds later the neonatal team rushed in, with Rebecca holding the baby in her hands.

As they set the infant on the O.R. table, the anesthesiologist put a tiny breathing tube in place. As soon as the airway was secured, the circulating nurse quickly scrubbed the chest as Dan took the scalpel and cleared his mind, focusing entirely on baby Erica and the complicated heart surgery she needed in order to stay alive.

Ten and a half hours later he lifted his head and stretched his neck muscles with a heavy sigh. It was over and Erica had come through the entire ordeal like a trouper.

He stared at the cardiac monitor, watching her heart rhythm flash across the screen in a fast but relatively steady beat. Her blood pressure was adequate, too, and there wouldn't be a better time to transfer her upstairs. "Call the NNICU and let them know she's coming up."

"Will do," one of the circulating nurses said.

He broke scrub, knowing the anesthesiologist would take care of the transfer. Erica would need to remain on the ventilator, not to mention on several different medications, as they waited for her body to heal from surgery. It was late now, not likely that Rebecca would still be around. No doubt she had someone else covering the evening shift.

As much as he wanted to head home, he knew he couldn't leave until he was certain little Erica was stable. The first few hours were the most critical, and if she started bleeding, he'd have to take her back to surgery.

He changed his scrubs and then took a few minutes to call Josh, as it was just past dinnertime. "Hi, Gemma, is Josh there?"

"Sure. I'll get him."

He could hear her yelling for Josh and soon his son picked up the phone. "Daddy? Are you coming home now?"

He closed his eyes and wished more than anything that he could go home just for a few minutes to give Josh a hug. "Not yet. But if everything goes well, I'll be home before you go to bed."

"Promise?" Josh asked.

He hesitated, hating to promise anything he couldn't deliver. "Josh, I promise that I'll try very hard to get home before you go to bed. A lot depends on how well my patient is doing. Okay?"

"Okay." Josh sounded distant, and Dan wished more than anything he could have had this last week at home. But at the same time tetralogy of Fallot, complicated by hypoplastic pulmonary arteries, was his specialty. Erica had the best chance with him as her surgeon.

As always, the tug between doing what was best for his patients and what was best for his son was difficult to navigate. He didn't want to let either of them down.

But when he did, it was invariably his son who suffered the most.

"How was therapy today?" he asked in an effort to prolong the conversation.

"Good."

Another one-word answer. He strove for patience and tried again. "Let's see if I can guess what flavor lollipop you chose for today. Hmm," he murmured dragging out the suspense as he pretended to ponder. "Cherry? No, I bet it was root beer."

There was a gasp. "How did you know it was root beer?" Josh demanded with awe.

Dan grinned. "I have superhuman powers," he teased. Glancing at his watch, he realized baby Erica was already up in the NICU by now. "Look, Josh, I have to go and check on my patient. I'll try to be home in a couple of hours, okay?"

"Okay. Good night, Daddy." At least this time he sounded as if he meant it.

"Good night, Josh." After Josh hung up, he stared at his phone for a moment, before slipping it into his pocket and heading over to the elevator. He always hoped and prayed his patients did well after surgery, especially since they were so small and vulnerable.

But this time he hoped and prayed twice as hard because he didn't want to disappoint his son.

He had been wrong about Rebecca, who was still there, and he found her studying Erica's lab results intently. "Hi, Dan," she said, somewhat distractedly.

"Rebecca. How's she doing?"

"Good so far. Her hemoglobin is stable for the moment."

"Glad to hear it." If Erica's hemoglobin stayed stable, he'd make it home in time to say good-night to Josh after all.

"I can watch her, if you want to head home," Rebecca offered. "I have to be here, anyway."

It was tempting, oh, so tempting to take her up on her offer but his rule was to wait for a least an hour. If patients were going to start bleeding it was generally within the first hour or two.

"I'll wait." He settled in a chair next to Erica's isolette.

"Your choice." She dropped next to him and they spent the next hour monitoring Erica's vital signs and lab values.

"This baby girl is a true star," Rebecca said, pushing away from the isolette well over an hour later. "Go home, Dan. Your son needs you."

He didn't have to be told twice. Erica did indeed look like a star. Or at least she was stable. And he didn't live far from the hospital if something happened later.

He crossed the threshold of his home fifteen minutes later, giving him thirty minutes before Josh usually went to bed. "Josh? Gemma? I'm home."

"Gemma's not here, Daddy," Josh said, wheeling into the living room.

His jaw dropped and his heart squeezed in panic. "What do you mean, she's not here?" he said in alarm. "Are you telling me she actually left you here all alone?"

"No, she didn't leave him alone." A female voice from the doorway made him swing round in shocked surprise. Molly stood there, looking wonderful. And nervous. "I—um—agreed to come over as she had to leave. Something about her daughter needing to go to the hospital."

"You did?" He stared at her, tempted to rush over and haul her into his arms, to prove she was real. Because having Molly waiting for him was something he'd secretly coveted.

"Yes. I hope you don't mind."

God, no, of course he didn't mind. In fact, this just might be the best news of his entire day. He reverently hoped Erica would remain stable back at the hospital as he flashed a grateful smile and gently closed the door behind him. "I don't mind at all."

CHAPTER TWELVE

MOLLY TRIED TO HIDE HER uncertainty about agreeing to come over to pinch-hit for Josh's nanny. Deep down, she'd figured this was a bad idea, but she hadn't been able to refuse Gemma, as the nanny's daughter had been taken to the hospital with suspected appendicitis.

She sat on the corner of Josh's bed, listening as Dan read Josh a bedtime story. Dan was doing a pretty good job, changing his voice to match the characters.

After the story, Josh wanted to hug and kiss both of them good-night. Dan went first, and then she stepped forward. As she bent over, giving him a hug and a kiss, and receiving the same in return, she couldn't help remembering how she'd often done the same thing with James's boys. She tried to tell herself this was different, but at the moment she had an undeniable sense of déjà vu.

"Molly, I don't know how to thank you for coming over on the spur of the moment like this," Dan said huskily, after he'd closed the door for Josh's room and led the way into the living room. "I owe you, big-time."

She forced herself to relax and smile. "It's no problem. Gemma was so upset about her daughter needing emergency surgery, there was no way I could turn her down. Besides, you know I care about Josh."

"Something I'm very grateful for," he said humbly.

She was secretly relieved he didn't seem to think she was chasing after him, considering the night they'd spent together. It had been her biggest fear in agreeing to cover for Gemma. Fortunately, the moment Dan had realized she was there, he'd looked happy to see her.

Still, she couldn't help wondering why Dan had left her name and number to use in case of an emergency in the first place. She didn't want to think that he was taking advantage of her.

She smiled, determined to leave on a friendly note. "Well, now that you're here, I'll head home. Good night, Dan."

"No, wait." He stepped forward and took her arm. "I'm sorry, Molly, but I was planning on Gemma spending the night in the guest room, in case I'm called back to the hospital."

She tried to hide her dismay. Of course, Gemma hadn't mentioned that small detail. "Even after working all day, you're still on call?"

"I have to be available in case Erica needs to be taken back to surgery," he explained patiently. "She's still in a very critical condition, after being taken to surgery mere moments after she was born."

Her eyes widened in shock. "Really? I had no idea that was even possible."

"It's not something we have to do often, but her case was very complicated. Only a few pediatric cardiothoracic surgeons in the country do this particular procedure."

And Dan Morris was one of them, she thought with a tiny thrill of pride. But then reality sank in and she glanced around with a sigh. "I didn't pack an overnight bag."

"There's plenty of extra toiletries here." he said gently. Before she could respond, he surprised her by coming forward to pull her into his arms. "I've missed you, Molly," he murmured before taking possession of her mouth in a deep kiss.

Her ability to think was severely hampered

by the way he kissed her so thoroughly. She soon became lost in his embrace. He'd actually started tugging her toward the bedroom and, heaven help her, she wasn't resisting when his phone rang.

"Dammit," he muttered, pulling away from her to fumble for his phone. "Yeah? Hi, Rebecca, what's going on?"

Molly took several deep breaths and smoothed her hair, trying to calm her erratic pulse, as she listened to the one-sided conversation. She'd managed to convince herself that a relationship between them was impossible, yet one kiss and she'd been ready to toss her fears and insecurities aside.

She must be going crazy. Granted, he'd called her on Sunday, but by the time they'd talked, she'd already convinced herself she must get over him.

Now she wasn't sure what to do.

"Okay, give her ten ccs of blood to run over an hour and I'll be there in ten—fifteen minutes tops."

She tried to hide her dismay. "Has the baby taken a turn for the worse?" she asked when he'd hung up.

"Not terrible, but she has been bleeding, so I really need to go in to see how she's doing."

His dark brown eyes were full of regret. "I'm sorry, Molly."

"That's okay, I understand," she said lightly. And she truly did understand. Clearly a tiny life hung in the balance. She would do a lot for her patients, too.

He came over and gave her another hard kiss, before turning back toward the door. But then he paused and glanced over his shoulder at her. "I don't expect you to wait up for me, because I don't know when I'll be back." He hesitated, and then added, "Make yourself at home, either in my bed or in the guest room. Wherever you're most comfortable." He said the last few words in a rush, and then left without waiting for a response.

She stared at the door long after he'd gone. Did he really mean what she thought he'd meant? That if she wanted to pick up their relationship where they'd left off on the weekend, she could sleep in his bed? Or if she wanted privacy and or distance she could use the guest room?

And what about Josh? He was old enough that he probably wouldn't wake up in the middle of the night and his inability to walk meant he wouldn't wander into Dan's room. Still, Josh could get up early and use the wheelchair to come in. Or would Dan expect her to sneak out in the morning before Josh was up?

She collapsed on the sofa and stared at the ceiling, her thoughts in turmoil. What was the right answer? What should she do?

No matter how badly she wanted to, she couldn't come to terms with the idea of crawling into Dan's bed. Not while Josh was so close.

But she didn't go into the guest room, either, worried that she might send the wrong message. Instead, she took her book and settled in the corner of the sofa, using a quilt for warmth. Soon the book slipped from her grasp, falling to the floor with a soft thud as she drifted into sleep.

"Daddy, shouldn't we wake her up?" Josh asked in a loud whisper.

Molly shifted and let out a low moan at the shaft of pain that shot through her neck from sleeping at an awkward angle. She prised her eyes open and found Josh's face scant inches from hers.

"Good morning," she murmured as she tried to unwrap herself from the quilt cocoon. She lifted her gaze to Dan, who stared at her with an enigmatic expression that she couldn't interpret. "Hi. How's your patient?"

A smile curved his mouth, softening his expression. "She's a true champ. Thankfully, she stabilized enough that I didn't have to take her back to the O.R."

"I'm so glad," she said, truly happy that the tiny newborn was doing so well. "Um, what time is it?"

"Six forty-five. I wasn't sure how long to let you sleep, because I didn't know if you had an eight o'clock patient or not."

"Six forty-five?" She shot up to her feet, having momentarily forgotten that today was Wednesday, a work day. "I don't—you're my first appointment of the day, but I still have to get ready."

"I'll make breakfast while you shower," Dan offered. She belatedly noticed that he must have already done that as his short hair gleamed with dampness.

"Thanks." She didn't like the thought of putting her same clothes back on, but at least she had a spare set of scrubs at work for emergencies like when a patient threw up or bled all over the place. She would have to make do with what she had.

But as she washed her hair in the shower,

she couldn't help wondering what time Dan had gotten home, and if he'd been disappointed when he'd noticed she hadn't chosen the option of sleeping in his bed.

And why she cared so much in wanting to know.

Dan suppressed a yawn as he drank more coffee, trying to compensate for fewer than three hours of sleep. He couldn't deny having been sorely disappointed to come home at two-thirty in the morning to find Molly asleep on the sofa. Fantasies of coming home to nuzzle her awake for some gentle lovemaking had instantly dissolved in a puff of smoke.

He'd stared at her for several seconds, tempted to lift her up and carry her to the guest bedroom, but then worried he'd only wake her up. So he'd left her alone, the way she'd apparently preferred, and gone to bed.

Where he'd wasted a precious thirty minutes he could have been sleeping, with tossing and turning and missing her.

Josh had woken him up at six, which was good because he hadn't been sure what time Molly needed to be at Angel's. And he'd taken time to do a quick check on Erica.

It wasn't until he'd started making breakfast that he'd realized that if Molly had slept with him, Josh would have come in to see them together. Not exactly something that would make him a candidate for father of the year.

The knot of tension between his shoulder blades eased, as he convinced himself that obviously that possibility had been what had caused Molly to avoid making herself comfortable in his room. Once again she'd proved she knew more than he did about kids, as he hadn't even considered that possibility until now.

And, worse, he suspected she might think less of him for even suggesting it.

For a moment he braced his hands on the counter and stretched the kinks from his neck. Being a single father in a relationship was much harder than he'd anticipated. Thankfully, Molly seemed to roll with the punches.

"I'll give you a back rub if you return the favor," she said from behind him. "My neck is killing me."

He swung round to face her. "I'll take you up on that offer any time," he said in a low voice. Just the thought of her hands on him made him tighten with need.

"What's for breakfast?" The way she shied away from the subject helped cool his desire.

"Just cereal today, hot or cold. Josh wants maple and brown sugar oatmeal."

"Sounds good to me. Make that a double."

"I'll make it a triple, since that's easiest all the way around. Just give me a few minutes to heat it up."

"I'll get the brown sugar, if you tell me where to find it," she offered.

"Third cupboard on your left." Within ten minutes they all sat down at the table and he was struck by the fact that even that first year, when Josh had just been a baby, he and Suzy had rarely shared breakfast.

Maybe an indication their marriage had been doomed from the start.

"If you want to drop me and Josh off at the physical therapy gym, we can start the session while you check on your patient," she offered.

"That would be great, thanks." As they finished their meal and then worked together to take care of the dishes, he wondered if this was how other families lived.

Or if this was just another of his fantasies that had no basis in reality?

* * *

Dan left Molly and Josh in the therapy gym and headed up to the NNICU to see Erica.

He found Erica's parents wrapped tightly in each other's arms, gazing at their tiny daughter in the isolette.

For a moment he had to look away. The love in their gazes was so intensely private, he felt like the worst kind of intruder. But he couldn't stand here forever, he had to check on their daughter's progress, so he cleared his throat and stepped forward.

"Dr. Morris," Jennifer greeted him tearfully, breaking away from her soldier husband. "Thank you for saving our daughter's life. This is my husband, Sergeant Eric Thompson."

Her husband was still wearing the fatigues he must have worn on the flight home. Dan stepped forward and offered his hand. "Pleased to meet you, Sergeant."

"I'm the lucky one," the young man said, shaking his hand. "I have you to thank for saving my family."

Uncomfortable with the praise, Dan brushed it aside. "Your daughter is a fighter. She's doing great. If she stays this good over the next twenty-four to forty-eight hours, we'll be able to get that breathing tube out."

"That would be wonderful," Jennifer said. "I want to hold her in my arms."

He understood. Obviously putting gloved hands through the windows of the isolette to touch their baby wasn't nearly as satisfying. "Soon," he promised. It was on the tip of his tongue to remind them that Erica would need more surgery down the road, but he decided there was plenty of time to broach that subject after they'd successfully gotten through this crisis.

According to the electronic medical record, Erica's vital signs were stable. She hadn't lost any more blood and the rest of her labwork was good. He used his pediatric stethoscope and reached through the windows of the isolette to listen to Erica's heart and lungs.

Satisfied the baby girl was holding her own, he stepped away. "She's doing fine," he said to reassure her parents. "I'm going to order some weaning parameters later on this afternoon, to see if we can turn the ventilator down a few notches."

"Thank you," Eric murmured, hugging his wife close.

Dan wrote the orders, chatted with Rebecca's replacement and then looked for Erica's nurse. He scowled a bit when he didn't recognize her and glanced at the nametag she wore on her scrubs. "Scarlet?" he asked. "Are you new here?"

"Yes, I'm the new head nurse, but I'm taking care of patients today." She wore her chocolate-brown hair pulled back from her face, and jutted her chin stubbornly. "Why, do you have a problem with that?"

"Depends on how well you do your job," he said, refusing to back down. "Marcus is covering for me, but if Erica takes a turn for the worse, I want you to call me directly, okay?"

"No problem. And don't worry—I have a lot of experience with neonates. I promise Erica is in good hands."

He gave a terse nod and turned away because he believed her. And it was time to pick up Josh.

As he left he glanced back at the young couple at Erica's isolette, impressed once again at how they physically and emotionally supported each other through this difficult time.

Would they make it over the long haul? Or would the endless toil and stress of life with a sick child eventually force them to part?

Cynically, he assumed the latter.

Then he stopped and turned back one more time to watch the young couple. Maybe, just maybe he needed to give them the benefit of the doubt. Just because he'd never experienced the type of love that lasted forever, it didn't mean that type of love didn't exist.

Molly was just finishing up with Josh's therapy when Dan arrived. She glanced up at him while she was running the ultrasound machine. "How's your patient?"

He was touched by her concern. Suzy had resented his pediatric patients, treating them like annoying inconveniences. "Much better. Should be able to start weaning her off the ventilator soon."

"That's wonderful. I'm sure her parents are relieved."

They were, so he nodded, but he didn't say anything more as he couldn't really talk about his patients much. All those privacy rules tended to get in the way. "How are you doing, Josh?" he asked, turning his attention to his son.

"We had fun. And I stood up again, right, Molly?"

"Yes, you did," she agreed with a soft

smile. It struck him in that moment how much she'd bonded with his son. "Your muscles are getting stronger every day."

"I'm glad." He took a seat on a stool next to Josh. "I'm sorry I couldn't be here this morning, Josh."

"That's okay," Josh said pragmatically. "Molly told me there's a baby with a sick heart that you need to take care of. That's way more important."

His chest tightened and he slowly shook his head. "No, that's not true. I do have to take care of kids that have sick hearts, but they're not more important than you, Josh. You're the most important thing in my life. But sometimes I do have to take care of sick kids, like today. Especially because I knew that you'd be okay here with Molly for a little while. But I want you to know that I'll always love you best."

"All finished," she said, and then shut off the ultrasound machine. "I, um, have to check on something. Excuse me." She hurried out of the room, without even wiping the gooey gel off Josh's legs.

Dan took the towel and did the task himself. "You're not mad at me, are you, Josh?" he finally asked, breaking the silence.

"No. I think I understand."

He was tempted to spring the news about the surprise birthday party on Saturday, but forced himself to keep silent. The look on Josh's face would be well worth the wait.

"What flavor lollipop do you want today?" he asked, reaching for the candy jar.

For a moment Josh simply stared at the various flavors. Then he turned his head up to face him. "What's your favorite flavor, Daddy?"

He was touched that his son cared enough to ask. "Lime. The green ones are my favorite."

"Then I'm going to have a green one," Josh said, digging his little fist in the jar until he grabbed a lime sucker. He ripped off the wrapper and stuck the candy into his mouth.

Dan glanced toward the doorway and saw Molly hovering there. He realized she'd purposefully left them alone to give them time to talk.

"So I'll see you tomorrow, then," she said lightly, as Josh levered himself into his wheelchair.

"Don't forget about Friday night," Dan said, following her out into the hallway so Josh couldn't overhear.

She froze and then shook her head. "Look, Dan, I don't think Friday is a good idea," she said, avoiding his gaze.

He frowned and glanced back to make sure Josh was still preoccupied. "Why not?"

She took a deep breath. "I came over last night to help out because you and Josh needed me, but I don't want to be a convenient surrogate nanny. Been there, done that, don't want to do it again."

He was startled by her revelation. "I want to see you, alone, Molly. Certainly not as a surrogate nanny. And I had no idea Gemma was planning to call you."

"Yet she did, because you left my name and number to be used in case of an emergency."

He couldn't quite hide the flash of guilt, but he wanted to know more about this previous relationship of hers. "What do you mean, been there, done that?"

"The last guy I dated was also a single father, and he used me as a surrogate mother for his boys all the time. Yet when I thought he was going to propose, he told me he loved someone else. He never cared about me the way he should have."

That guy was just plain stupid, he thought, but managed to keep it to himself. "But I haven't been doing that with you, Molly. I do care about you. I want to take you to dinner so we can spend some time alone. I swear to you, making you a surrogate nanny was never my intention."

But she shook her head, not giving an inch. "Dan, I'll help you with…Saturday's plans because I promised I would, but that's all. I have to go, my next patient is waiting."

And before he could protest or ask anything more, she turned and walked away.

CHAPTER THIRTEEN

MOLLY TRIED TO ERASE the stricken expression on Dan's face from her mind, but it stuck with her as she worked with her patients throughout the day.

Logically, she knew she'd made the right decision. Getting involved with Dan hadn't been very smart in the first place. She should have known better than to make the same mistakes she'd made with James.

Wasn't he already using her as a replacement nanny? Soon he'd leave her at home with Josh while he went out on dates. She had no doubt he'd find someone else to fall in love with, breaking her heart in the process. Just like James had done.

The organ in question ached in her chest as she rode the subway home. The newspaper she'd brought along to read didn't even come close to holding her attention.

Two more days of therapy and then Josh's birthday party on Saturday. After that, she probably wouldn't see Dan anymore. He'd go back to work full time, as Josh had gotten through the worst of his crisis. She'd continue to see Josh as a patient, but wouldn't see Dan. Wouldn't be forced to make small talk with him, as if she wasn't slowly bleeding to death inside.

She loved him.

The realization made her blink in surprise, although now that she'd admitted it she was surprised she'd fooled herself for this long.

She loved him. She loved the way he'd turned his relationship with his son around. She loved the way he cared about his tiny patients. She loved the way she could make him smile and laugh.

And most of all she loved the way he centered his intenseness on her when they were alone, as if she was the only person on the planet who mattered.

But they hadn't been alone together much. The night of Jack's going-away party and the night he'd taken her to dinner. Two nights out of two weeks.

Ridiculous to think she could fall in love in

such a short time. She cared about Dan, but love? How could that be?

She didn't know how it had happened, but it had. She loved him or she wouldn't be so upset about leaving him.

She got off the subway at her stop, holding the newspaper she hadn't read over her head when it started raining. She shivered and practically ran the rest of the way to her apartment.

Inside, she quickly changed out of her damp clothes into a pair of warm sweats. When her phone rang, she leaped to answer it, trying not to be too disappointed when she recognized the caller as her sister. "Hi, Sally, how are you?"

"Great, I'm great. Hey, listen, I know I should have asked you about this earlier, but will you be one of my bridesmaids at my wedding?"

Molly hesitated, wanting nothing more than to be included, but she knew her sister really would rather have one of her friends.

"I'm sorry I didn't ask you sooner," Sally said in a rush, filling the awkward silence. "And I don't blame you for being upset. I ran into your boyfriend in the cafeteria yesterday and he told me I should be ashamed at how I'm always taking you for granted. That I should be grateful for having a sister. And he's right. I am grateful, Molly. So will you please consider standing up with me at my wedding?"

Tears burned her eyelids as her heart swelled with joy. "Yes, Sally, of course I will. I'd love to be a bridesmaid at your wedding."

"Oh, I'm so glad, Molly. Thank you." She thought it must be her imagination because she thought she heard Sally sniffling on the other end of the line. "We're going shopping for dresses a week from Saturday. Do you want to come along? That is, if you don't have other plans."

"I'd love to come along, and of course I don't have other plans." She was still reeling from the knowledge that Dan had approached Sally at work, just to stick up for her. And she was glad they weren't shopping this weekend, as this Saturday was Josh's birthday. "Let me know what time and what store you're planning to meet at."

"I haven't figured that out yet," Sally admitted. "But I will soon. Thanks again, Molly. I love you."

Her heart almost folded in half at the second shocker of the day. "I love you, too," she managed to choke out.

"Bye, Molly." After her sister had hung up, she stared at the phone for several moments before she set it down, grinning like a fool. She'd mentally prepared herself to be left out of the wedding party, had even wondered if she'd make the invite list. But thanks to Dan, Sally had realized that being sisters was important.

Maybe their relationship wouldn't be completely fixed overnight, but this was a good start. A really, really good start.

Her smile faded. She wondered who in Dan's life had made him aware of how important he was? Certainly not his ex-wife. And he didn't have any brothers or sisters, because he'd mentioned being an only child.

The ache in her heart returned, and she wondered if she'd been too hasty in her refusal to see Dan again.

Molly looked for opportunities to have a personal conversation with Dan, but as the week went on she hardly saw him at all. According to Josh, his dad had been on call again, leaving Mitch to spend the night and subsequently accompany Josh to therapy.

She should have been glad to hear Dan hadn't used her as one of his nannies but instead she couldn't help feeling guilty at how she'd left things between them.

Telling herself that putting distance between them was for the better was one thing. But the lingering doubts wouldn't go away.

After rain during the week, the sun came out by Friday and according to the weather reports, temperatures were supposed to get up as high as sixty degrees by Saturday. Perfect weather for Josh's surprise birthday party and the wheelchair football game.

She'd been thrilled to see Dan on Friday afternoon, but he was all business as they stored the wheelchairs in the truck he'd rented.

"That's the last of them," he said, stepping down from the truck. "Thanks for your help, Molly."

She tried to smile, even though she missed the easy camaraderie that they'd once shared. "No problem. I'm going to head out to the park early to hide the prizes. What time are you going to have Josh there?"

"The party starts at one, so I thought we'd get there about one-fifteen." They'd already agreed that the other kids should all be there, holding a big birthday banner, before Josh arrived. "Unless you think we need to wait a little longer?" he asked uncertainly.

She pursed her lips, considering the time-frame. "No, I think one-fifteen should be fine. I suspect some of the kids will get there early, anyway."

Dan reached out to take her hand in his. "Molly, I've been thinking a lot about what you said earlier this week. If you don't want to help me with this party, I can handle it on my own," he said, his eyes dark and serious. "I don't want you to think I'm taking advantage of you."

"You're not taking advantage. I want to help. I want to be there for Josh." Seeing him now, after missing him for several days, she wondered if she'd been wrong to compare him to James. "Besides, I owe you for the way you stood up for me with my sister. She told me what you said to her in the cafeteria."

Dan scowled. "She needed to hear the truth. But that doesn't matter, because there isn't a score card, Molly. Friends help friends without expecting anything in return."

"I know." She kept the smile on her face, even though she feared her cheeks might crack from the pressure. Her instincts were screaming at her that she'd been wrong, but this wasn't the time or the place to discuss their personal issues.

He let out a heavy sigh. "I have to go, but I hope maybe after Josh's party you and I can talk. There are…some things I'd like to share with you."

Now he'd intrigued her. "All right."

He flashed a lopsided grin and then nodded. "See you tomorrow, Molly."

"Until then, Dan." She couldn't understand the sudden sadness that nearly overwhelmed her when he walked away.

She had trouble falling asleep that night, thinking too much about Dan and Josh, and then overslept. When she realized it was almost ten in the morning, she shot out of bed like a rocket.

Thankfully, she'd already wrapped her present for Josh, hoping he'd like the Yankees sweatshirt she'd bought him, a miniature replica of his father's. She'd been tempted to get the full uniform, but since she knew he wouldn't be playing much this year, she'd chosen the sweatshirt instead.

But she still had dozens of gifts to hide near where they were going to play wheelchair football. She quickly showered and changed her clothes. Once she was ready, she tossed the items in a large reusable grocery bag and then headed down to the subway.

The ride to Central Park didn't take long, and she relaxed when she realized she had almost two full hours to get the gifts hidden and the banner ready. Hiding the gifts didn't take long, and she spent some of her extra time lining up the wheelchairs into two teams.

As she'd suspected, several kids came early. "Where's Josh and his dad?" the first mom asked, craning her neck as if to search him out.

"They're not here yet. He's bringing Josh at one-fifteen. The party is a surprise."

"Oh." Her face fell in disappointment.

Molly tried not to scowl at how the woman was clearly interested in Dan, considering she'd shown up at the birthday party dressed to kill in cream slacks and a red blouse that dipped low enough in the front to show off a fair amount of cleavage.

"I guess I can wait, then."

Molly's gaze narrowed but she simply shrugged. "Suit yourself."

"What did you say your name was again?" the woman asked as she turned to greet the next child.

"Molly Shriver." Maybe it was small of her, but she didn't label herself as Josh's physical therapist. She turned to the next new arrival. "Hi, welcome to Josh's surprise party. Thanks so much for coming."

By ten after one a large crowd of kids had gathered in the park in front of the wheel-chairs. Molly took charge, unrolling the banner and getting all the kids together to hold it up for Josh.

When Dan and Josh arrived, Josh's eyes widened in shock as everyone yelled, "Surprise!"

"Happy birthday, Josh," Dan said, as he got Josh's wheelchair out of the trunk. "Guess what? We're going to play wheelchair football."

"We are?" Josh looked as if he was shell-shocked as the kids crowded around and wished him happy birthday before picking out their own wheelchairs.

"We are," Molly said, crossing over to give him a hug. "And you're going to have the advantage in this game," she whispered, giving him a secret wink. "You know how to use your wheelchair, they don't."

"Oh, yeah!" Josh's eyes glittered with excitement.

"Dan? Hi, Dan, remember me? Stephanie Albert?" The woman in the cream-colored slacks that were distinctly out of place here at the park came rushing over.

"Oh, uh, yeah, sure," Dan said in a vague, distracted tone. "It was nice of you to bring your son to Josh's party."

"Well, of course I brought him. He's friends with Josh, isn't he?" The way Stephanie beamed up at Dan made Molly curl her hands into fists. Not that she had any right to be upset.

Or jealous.

"Hey, Molly, what do you think? Should we act as referees?" Dan asked, as the kids started piling into their wheelchairs.

She hid a grin as the nicely dressed woman wrinkled her nose in distaste. Clearly she wasn't offering to referee, the way she'd dressed. "Sounds good. We can each coach one of the teams, too."

"Excellent plan," Dan said, ignoring Stephanie as if she didn't exist. "I brought us whistles," he said, handing her one of the shiny metal whistles on a chain. "Let's go."

"I'll pick up Craig later," Stephanie called out, as if desperate for one last fragment of attention.

Dan lifted his hand, but didn't turn around

so he didn't see the way Stephanie frowned and stomped away, like a spoiled little kid who hadn't gotten her way.

But Molly sensed that the woman had only retreated for the moment. It was clear she had every intention of trying to be the next Mrs. Doctor Dan Morris.

A plot that Dan seemed completely oblivious to. Which made her feel ridiculously happy as she hurried after Dan onto the football field.

Dan couldn't have asked for a better day for Josh's birthday party, and he had nearly as much fun as his son. The look of excitement in Josh's eyes was worth every minute of the seemingly endless preparations.

"Go, Josh, go!" he shouted, when his son went racing out toward the end zone for a pass.

"Get him!" Molly screamed to her team, but it was too late. Josh caught the ball and then rolled in for the winning touchdown.

"Way to go, Josh," Dan shouted again, all attempt at being impartial gone. "Way to go!"

Molly threw up her hands in disgust, but she didn't look too upset when she went over to give Josh a high five.

"This was too hard," Craig Albert said, letting go of his wheelchair wheels in a deep sulk. "We should have played regular football."

Dan had to bite his tongue to stop himself from pointing out it was Josh's party, and Josh couldn't play regular football. He did his best to ignore Craig's whining. "Good game, everybody, good game," he said, slapping his hands against each team member's in a high five.

"There are prizes hidden around the park," Molly said, when the kids had gathered in the center of the football field. "You might want to stay in your wheelchairs to find them and there's one for each of you, so once you find a prize, you need to come back here, okay?"

"Yay, prizes!" Craig rolled across the grass, but then was the first to abandon his wheelchair, so that he could look for the best hiding places.

"That kid grates on my nerves," Dan muttered to Molly, keeping his tone low so that the other kids couldn't hear him.

"Really? I thought you were friends with his mother?"

He stared at her in shock. "Are you crazy?

That viper? Where do you think that poor kid gets his attitude from?"

She laughed and he basked in the musical sound for a moment.

"I've missed you, Molly," he said softly. "You have no idea how much."

Her laughter died away and she looked down as if she felt guilty. "I know, because I missed you, too."

Her words gave him a flash of hope. Maybe he hadn't totally ruined things between them after all? He tried to think of a way to help her understand. "Look, Molly, I know I'm not very good at being in a relationship, and I'm sure I've already made tons of mistakes, but I'd like you to give me another chance. I think, no, I'm sure I can do better."

She glanced up at him, surprise reflected on her features. "Dan, you haven't made any big mistakes, not really. It was my fault. I shouldn't have overreacted."

"You didn't overreact, you had every right to be upset." When she'd mentioned how the jerk who'd left her had two sons and had used her as a surrogate mother, he'd been extremely angry. And desperate to prove he wasn't doing the same thing. "I care about you, Molly. But I'm not sure how to show you. It's been a long time…" He stopped, unwilling to admit how ignorant he really was.

What did he know about love? He hadn't ever experienced it before. Not until Molly.

Stunned, he felt his heart squeeze in his chest. Was he really falling in love with Molly?

"Oh, Dan," she murmured, but then stopped whatever she'd been about to say when Josh came wheeling over.

"Daddy! Craig has two prizes and Amy is crying because she doesn't have one."

"Figures," he muttered. When the sound of Amy crying grew louder, he broke into a jog. "Don't leave yet, I'll be right back," he called over his shoulder, resenting Craig for being a brat and for interrupting his conversation with Molly.

A conversation he had every intention of finishing before he let her slip away.

Thankfully, he needn't have worried. Molly didn't leave. In fact, she stayed, helping him serve twenty kids pizza, punch, cake and ice cream.

When it came time for Josh to open his presents, Dan watched with pride as his son did so with glee, tearing into one package after another. And when Craig tried to grab the remote control to Josh's new truck, he swiftly intervened, snatching it away and handing it back to Josh. "I think the birthday boy should be the first one to try it, don't you?" he asked through gritted teeth.

Craig went back to sulking, but Dan didn't care. And when the parents of the kids started to arrive, he wanted to weep with relief. Even Stephanie Albert was a welcome sight if nothing more than to get Craig out of his hair.

"Did you have fun, sweetie-pie?" Stephanie asked, ruffling her son's hair.

"Our team didn't win and he wouldn't let me play with the remote-control car," Craig said, shooting Dan a dark look.

If the kid thought he was going to apologize, he was wrong. "Thanks for coming," he said cheerfully. "And don't forget your prize."

Craig snatched the mini pinball machine he'd won and stalked off, with his mother trailing behind.

"Good riddance," Molly muttered.

"You have that right," he said with heartfelt relief.

More parents streamed in and soon everyone was gone. As the wheelchairs had been picked up earlier, the cleanup job didn't take long.

Dan stared at the stack of presents Josh

had accumulated. "I'm not sure we'll be able to fit all this in the trunk of my car, along with Josh's wheelchair," he muttered. But he'd rather cut off his arm than ask Molly for help, even though he wanted to finish their conversation more than he wanted to breathe.

"I'll help you. Between the two of us we'll get the car packed up, no problem," Molly said.

"Only if you're sure," he said, looking down into her bright green eyes. "There's no scorecard, Molly. If you want to go home, we'll handle it. You and I can always talk later."

Her tremulous smile tugged at his heart. "I know you can handle anything, but I'd like to help, if you'll have me."

Have her? Little did she know he wasn't about to let her go without a fight.

CHAPTER FOURTEEN

MOLLY WAS IN AWE OF HOW well Dan had handled the wheelchair football game, along with the subsequent meal for Josh's party, especially the not-so-nice kids like Craig Albert. Scary how much that kid was like his mother.

Just thinking of the way Dan had stared at her in horror when she'd mentioned Stephanie Albert made her feel warm and gooey inside. Clearly, he wasn't attracted to the woman, not even one little bit. And he wanted a second chance.

With her.

And, heaven help her, she wanted that, too.

She let out a little sigh of relief when Dan pulled into the parking garage beneath his fancy high-rise apartment building. "You don't have to carry those," he protested, when she gathered a bunch of Josh's presents into her arms. "I can make a few trips."

The way he was falling over himself trying not to take advantage of her made her smile. "Dan, it's fine. No scorecard, remember?" she chided lightly.

He grimaced and pulled Josh's wheelchair out, before loading up on gifts and leading the way to the elevator. Josh wheeled himself alongside, with his remote-controlled truck sitting on his lap, as if he wasn't about to be parted from the gift. She'd noticed that one was from Dan, and she silently approved of his choice. Perfect for now, with Josh being wheelchair bound, yet something he could still use once he was walking again.

Once inside Dan's home, they stacked the gifts in the corner of Josh's room.

"You realize you need to write thank-you notes for these," she said to Josh.

He wrinkled his nose, his face falling in dismay. "I do?"

"Yes. You do." She fought a grin as Dan sighed heavily at the news. "I'm sure your dad can get them to your teacher, who can hand them out to the kids at school."

"We'll work on them tomorrow, Josh," Dan assured him. "The sooner we get them done, the better."

"That's probably best." She glanced around,

and noticed that Josh was bending over in his wheelchair, trying to massage his calf muscles. "What's wrong?"

"My legs are sore," Josh admitted.

"Really?" Dan scowled a bit and knelt beside his son's wheelchair to feel his legs. "That's strange because we didn't play the ball game very long this morning. I would think your arms would be sore after the game of wheelchair football, not your legs."

"Actually, using a wheelchair does exercise the core muscles along with the upper arms," she felt compelled to point out. "But even with that, it's possible Josh was unconsciously tightening his leg muscles while he played, especially when he was making those sharp turns on the field." She turned toward Josh. "You'd better let me massage them for you."

Dan looked relieved and nodded. "If you wouldn't mind, that would be great."

"Of course I don't mind." She helped Josh get settled on his bed while Dan brought in the bottle of lotion she'd used last time. "Do you have a heating pad?" she asked. "Heat helps to relax tense muscles, too."

"I'm not sure, I'll check."

As Dan went in search of the heating pad she instructed Josh to roll over on his stomach. She began to massage his lower legs, starting with the gastrocnemius and then moving onto the soleus, which was only slightly less tense.

"Feels good," Josh murmured groggily, as if he was half-asleep. She smiled, suspecting that the excitement of the day was catching up with him.

"I'm glad," she said, soothing the angry, tense muscles with her fingers. As before, his right leg was far worse than his left.

"I found it," Dan said in a low voice, bringing in the electric heating pad. He set it up while she finished the massage. She applied the heating pad to Josh's right leg and within moments the boy was out for the count, sound asleep.

She followed Dan from Josh's room, partially closing the door behind her. When they reached the living room, he surprised her by drawing her toward the sofa. "Please sit down for a moment."

She sat, knowing he meant to continue the conversation they'd started during Josh's party. She linked her fingers together to hide her nervousness.

He sat in the chair to her right so that he could face her. "Molly, there's so much I want to say to you, I don't even know where to start. First of all, thanks for everything you did today. Your idea for Josh's birthday party was brilliant. And I'll never forget the look on Josh's face when he saw all of you standing behind the banner, yelling, 'Surprise!'"

She couldn't help but smile. "The look on his face was priceless, wasn't it? And you did a lot of the work, too." She paused, and then added, "I'm so happy when I see how you and Josh are together now, compared to the day we first met. You've accomplished a minor miracle, Dan."

"You're the miracle, Molly," he said in a low, husky tone. "I owe everything to you."

"No, Dan, I'm sure you would have found your way back together again, even without my help." She lifted her gaze up to meet his. "You're a good father. You love Josh and I'm convinced your love can get you through anything."

"Molly." He reached over to rest the palm of his hand against her cheek. "You have to understand something. I don't really know much about love. My mother—well, let's just say I was a major inconvenience in her life. She never once let me forget how everything that was bad in our lives was my fault."

She felt herself pale, and brought up her hand to cover his. "That's terrible, Dan. How terrible of her to say those things to you!"

He rubbed his thumb across her cheek, but then pulled away, rising to his feet and turning his back as he began to pace. "Leaving home, going to college and then getting into medical school was the best thing I ever did. Everyone kept telling me what a great doctor I was, how much talent I had. I was at the top of my class, and then quickly rose to the top of my career. And when I met Suzy she claimed to adore me, so I married her."

He turned to face her, his gaze full of despair, and her heart ached for him. "But she didn't love me, she only wanted my money. I basically went from one loveless existence to another. Until Josh was born."

"I know you loved your son the moment you saw him," she murmured.

"Yes, I did. I do. I've been wrestling with guilt over the accident that put Josh in the wheelchair, even though I know the other driver was primarily at fault. Still, I've been trying hard to move forward."

"Dan, surely you realize that the accident might have happened even if you hadn't been distracted. The guy ran a red light, right?"

"Yes, you're right. And I'm getting better there, but I'm afraid that without you I'll fall back into my old patterns."

"You won't, Dan. I believe in you. And to be honest, I feel like having me around will only get in the way." Saying the words, remembering how Josh and Dan had looked as they'd wheeled themselves down to Central Park that day, made her realize why she needed to leave.

Now. Before she lost any more of her heart.

"What are you saying?" he asked hoarsely.

She steeled her resolve. "I'm saying you need to take the time to concentrate on your relationship with your son." She ignored the cracks rippling through her heart, breaking it into zillions of pieces. "Without allowing anything else getting in the way."

"Is that really what you think?" he asked, his face pale.

She forced herself to nod. "Yes, that is exactly what I think." She rose to her feet and forced herself to take a step toward the door. "I care about you and Josh. And I only want you to be happy."

"Don't go," he said, and the tortured expression on his face nearly brought her to her knees.

"I have to." She lifted one shoulder in a helpless shrug. "I'm sorry, Dan, but I think you need to come to grips with your past and your present before you can even begin to contemplate a future."

He froze, as if pierced by her words. And in that moment she knew her gut instincts were right.

He wasn't ready for a true give-and-take relationship. Wasn't ready to be vulnerable enough to fall in love. For a moment her resolve wavered, because she could see just how clearly he needed someone to love him.

The way she loved him.

Yet didn't she deserve that same love in return? She'd given herself to James and his sons, and for what? No, she couldn't bear to have her heart broken again.

So she turned and left his apartment, intent on taking the subway home. And she wasn't sure which hurt more. Leaving him when she so badly wanted to stay or the grim knowledge that he hadn't tried to stop her.

The moment Molly left, Dan stared at the closed door, feeling more alone than ever before in his entire life. Worse than when Suzy had left him with their one-year-old son.

But the truth in her words resonated deep within him. Maybe she was right. Maybe he did need to resolve his past and his present relationship with Josh, before he could contemplate a future.

She'd told him he was a good father, but he wasn't sure if that was really true. His relationship with Josh had come a long way, and he wasn't about to lose the ground they'd gained, but instinctively he knew that having Molly around wouldn't distract him. He fought a rising sense of despair. He needed Molly to help show him the way.

He needed Molly to love him.

The way his mother and Suzy hadn't.

He'd grown beyond his mother's bitterness, had managed to come out with a great career in spite of her, but for some reason Suzy's betrayal seemed worse. Because he'd stupidly believed she'd loved him, even though she hadn't.

He still resented her. For leaving him. For the way she'd spent his money and then tossed him aside as if he wasn't good enough.

For distracting him the day of the crash. A crash that had almost killed Josh and had left him in a wheelchair.

He sank onto the edge of the sofa, cradling

his head in his hands as bitter anger sloshed in his gut like bad whiskey. Maybe Molly was right. Maybe he needed to let go of his anger and resentment before he could move forward.

The image of baby Erica's parents holding each other, drawing strength from each other, as they'd sat next to the tiny isolette flashed into his mind. He remembered doubting the ability of their love to survive the stress of having a sick infant.

But maybe he had it backward. Maybe the reason his and Suzy's marriage had fallen apart after Josh's birth had been because they hadn't loved each other the way they should have in the first place.

Maybe true love held couples together during times of stress, rather than pulling them apart.

He'd known that things between him and Suzy hadn't been great even before Josh had been born. She'd made no secret of the fact that she'd hated everything about being pregnant. He'd hoped things would change once the baby was born, but instead they had gone from bad to worse.

He'd loved Josh the moment he'd first seen him, but he hadn't been an easy baby. Josh had suffered from colic and for those first few months he'd cried for hours on end.

Suzy hadn't been able to stand it, so he'd walked the floor with Josh, trying to soothe the colicky baby at night, while building his pediatric cardiothoracic practice during the day. He existed on little to no sleep, and it was by sheer luck he'd discovered that putting Josh in the baby swing and running the vacuum cleaner, of all things, had soothed his son more than anything else. Finally, they'd had at least a couple hours of peace and quiet.

Josh had grown out of his colicky phase by the time he was six months old, turning into a smiling, happy baby. But Suzy had still left just after Josh's first birthday. And he'd tried to manage on his own.

With his growing surgical practice he'd ended up spending less and less time at home, leaving Josh to the care of his nanny. Except for his days off, of course, when he'd had to haul Josh from one sporting event to another. Something he'd started to resent until that fateful crash, where he'd almost lost the one thing most precious to him.

Which brought him full circle, to the day he'd met Molly. The petite firecracker who'd dared to yell at him, had ordered him to get a wheelchair and who'd shown him the importance of having fun.

And what had she wanted in return? Nothing but for him to love his son.

No, wait. That wasn't exactly true. Over these past few weeks he'd learned a lot about Molly. He knew that deep down she wanted love and a family.

The knowledge hit him in the head like a brick. Of course Molly wanted love. She deserved love.

He was an idiot for not telling her how much he loved her!

He stood, and actually started for the door to follow Molly, before he remembered Josh was sleeping in his bed.

Spinning round, he went to find his phone. Okay, so he'd arrange for a babysitter. Josh might sleep the rest of the night anyway, and he wanted to talk to Molly. Now. Before it was too late.

Too late for what, he wasn't sure, but the sense of urgency wouldn't be denied.

He dialed Mitch's number, hoping and praying the college kid had another exam coming up. Or at the very least, wasn't already out partying on a Saturday night.

And if Mitch wasn't home, he'd call every

babysitter he knew until he found someone who would come over. Because he desperately needed to see Molly again.

She deserved to know the truth.

He loved her!

Molly was reading in bed, finding it difficult to focus on the murder mystery while trying not to think about Dan. When her apartment buzzer sounded, she started badly. With a frown she pulled on her robe over her pajamas and went over to the intercom. "Who is it?"

"It's Dan—will you please let me come up?"

Dan? What on earth was he doing here? She glanced helplessly over her shoulder at her messy apartment, but pushed the intercom button again. "Uh, sure. Come on up." She pushed the middle button, which unlocked the door, and then ran her fingers through her tousled hair.

She probably looked awful in her ratty robe and no makeup, but there wasn't time to make herself look presentable. Besides, why should she care what she looked like? She'd spent the last two hours trying to forget about Dan and Josh, convinced she'd done the right thing by walking away. Giving them the time they needed. That they deserved.

So why was he here?

He rapped on her apartment door, startling her from her thoughts. Full of apprehension, she opened the door. "Hi, is Josh okay?"

"He was still sleeping when I left." Dan stepped inside, forcing her back a few steps, and then closed the door behind him. "Thanks for letting me come up. I really need to talk to you."

She glanced at him uncertainly. "Dan, I'm not sure there's anything more to say—" she began.

"I love you," he interrupted.

She blinked, opened her mouth and then closed it again. Was she dreaming? She must be because she couldn't believe what she was hearing. Somehow she managed to find her voice. "Excuse me?"

"I love you." He took a step toward her, and she instinctively took a step back. "I love you, Molly Shriver. I know you think I need to concentrate on my relationship with my son, and I will. But I don't want to lose you, either."

Her knees went weak and she tried to wrap her mind around what he was saying. She desperately wanted to believe him, but what if she was wrong? "I don't understand."

"Then I can't be saying it right," he muttered, and before she realized what he was about to do he pulled her into his arms and slanted his mouth over hers in a hot, deep kiss.

She melted against him, wanting to be in his arms more than she wanted to breathe. When he lifted his head a few moments later, she swallowed a protest.

"I love you, Molly," he said again, for the fourth time. And, heaven help her, she was actually starting to believe him. No one, not even James, had ever looked so serious and sincere when saying those three little words. Dan's love beamed from his heart up to his eyes. "You've brought sunshine and joy back into my life. I know I don't deserve you, but I can't bear the thought of losing you."

The conviction in his voice and the expression of hope on his face shook her to the core. Here was this dear man who'd never had anyone love him offering his heart to her. She felt awed and humbled to be on the receiving end of such a gift. "Oh, Dan—you haven't lost me. I was only going to give you and Josh some time to be together, that's all." She realized that by walking out on him she'd done the same thing as his ex-wife. She couldn't prevent her eyes from filling with happy tears. "I love you, too, Dan. So much that it scares me."

"You do?" He looked almost afraid to believe her. "My career is time-consuming, but I want you to know that I plan to put my family first. You and Josh will always come first."

"I know your patients need you, Dan. Josh and I will always support you, no matter what, because we love you."

"Molly…" His voice broke and he swept her into his arms again, burying his face in her hair. "I love you so much."

Before she could say anything more he picked her up, strode into her bedroom and kicked the door shut behind them.

The next week passed in a blur as the work that had stacked up while Dan had been away now teetered over him like a potential avalanche. He didn't get nearly enough time to sneak over to share lunch with Molly or to get home in time to share dinner with Josh.

Thankfully, he wasn't on call the following weekend and was determined to make up for lost time with Molly and Josh by inviting her over for dinner on Friday night.

He was grateful to Gemma, who'd made a beautiful pan of lasagna, which meant all he had to do was to toss a salad together and open a bottle of wine.

He was nervous because he'd purchased an engagement ring and was planning to ask Molly to marry him. Tonight. Which was probably rushing it.

He should wait. But he didn't want to. He wanted the whole world to know she belonged to him.

When the door buzzer went, his heart leaped into his throat. "I'll get it," Josh shouted, as he hurled his wheelchair toward the door.

"Hi, Josh. Hi, Dan," Molly said, as she stepped into the living room.

Conscious of Josh's keen gaze, Dan gave her a quick kiss, despite how badly he wanted to linger. "Hi, Molly."

"Something smells delicious." Her warm gaze, full of love, settled his nerves. "What can I do to help?" she asked.

"Nothing. I have everything ready to go."

As they wandered into the kitchen, she asked his son about his day, listening intently as Josh described how he'd managed to pull a B on his latest math test. As Dan poured the wine and then started the salad, he found he enjoyed listening to them.

"Mitch helped me a lot," Josh said. "Some of the mistakes I made were stupid."

"Well, don't beat yourself up over them," she chided. "Just remember next time to go slowly and double-check your work."

As they sat down for dinner, Dan was struck by how much they already seemed like a family. His love for Molly overwhelmed him.

When they'd finished the meal, he took the dirty dishes into the kitchen, leaving Molly and Josh alone. When he returned a few minutes later he stopped in the doorway when he heard Molly talking to his son. "Josh, I have something very important to ask you."

"You do?" Josh's eyes widened, as if sensing the seriousness in her tone. Dan stood stock-still, just out of sight, wondering what she was about to say.

"Yes." Molly actually looked nervous as she took Josh's hand in hers. "Josh, I love you. And I love your dad. I want to ask you if you'll let me marry your dad and become your new mother."

"For real?" Josh whispered, his brown eyes growing even larger. "You're going to marry my dad and be my new mother?"

She nodded slowly. "If you'll let me."

"Yes! Of course we'll marry you!" Josh cried, and he launched himself at Molly, who caught him in a huge hug.

Dan watched them, his heart swelling with love, respect and pride. He stepped forward, capturing her gaze with his. "I think I'm the one who's supposed to pop the question," he murmured with a smile. He pulled out the small velvet box holding the engagement ring, opened it and slid it over to her on the table. "I was hoping to ask you later tonight."

"Really?" she gasped, and her eyes welled up with tears. "I'm sorry."

"Don't be." He reached over to pull the two most important people in his life close to his chest. "Just say yes."

"Yes," she whispered, burrowing close. "A thousand times, yes."

He smiled with satisfaction as he held his future.

His family.

EPILOGUE

Six months later...

DAN STOOD AT THE ALTAR of the small church that Molly's parents still attended regularly, waiting patiently for his bride to appear. Molly had chosen to have a smaller service, after her sister Sally's more lavish affair.

And he was fine with that. Molly knew, just as he did, that the ceremony was only the beginning. He caught a glimpse of white and held his breath. When the music swelled and everyone in the church rose to their feet, he stepped forward eagerly.

The two attendants came first, and he recognized Molly's sister, Sally, and her best friend, Kara. But he didn't spare them more than a second glance as he waited for Josh.

When he saw his son, standing right in front of Molly, on his own two feet, no wheelchair in sight, his chest tightened with a mixture of love and fear. Maybe they'd rushed this? What if Josh's legs weren't strong enough to hold him? What if he tripped and fell when walking up the aisle with the braces on his legs?

As Josh stepped forward, though, he realized he needn't have worried, because his son was smiling widely as he made his way down the center of the aisle, his gait clumsy with the braces but each deliberate step like music to his ears just the same. When Josh reached the front, he came over to stand right next to his dad.

"Good job, son," Dan murmured, putting his arm around Josh's shoulders. "I love you."

"I love you, too, Dad." Josh flashed him a broad smile but then focused his attention on watching his soon-to-be new mother, Molly, as she walked down the aisle toward them.

"She's so beautiful," Josh whispered.

"Yes, she is." And all his, he thought humbly as he moved forward to take Molly's arm, so they could approach the altar together. With Molly at his side, he could face anything the universe had in store for them. This was the beginning of a new life together.

As husband and wife. As a family with Josh.

And he knew, deep down, that their love would only grow stronger with each passing day.

* * * * *